CW01431231

Evette: A Domestic Thriller

Maternal Instincts

L.A. Detwiler

Published by L.A. Detwiler, 2022.

Maternal Instincts Series

Book One: The Delivery
Book Two: Evette
Novella (Free link when you buy The Delivery): The Labor
Other books by L.A. Detwiler
The Widow Next Door
The One Who Got Away
The Diary of a Serial Killer's Daughter
A Tortured Soul
The Redwood Asylum
The Christmas Bell
The Arsonist's Handbook
The Flayed One
Short Stories by L.A. Detwiler
"Mirrored"
"Slaughtered Love"
"The Christmas Bell: Rachel's Story"
"It Started on Halloween"
"Her Darkest Hour"
"The Witch of War Creek"

Copyright © 2022 by L.A. Detwiler

All rights reserved. This book or any portion thereof may not be reproduced or used in any manner whatsoever without the express written permission of the publisher except for the use of brief quotations in a book review.

This is a work of fiction. Names, characters, businesses, places, events, locales, and incidents are either the products of the author's imagination or used in a fictitious manner. Any resemblance to actual persons, living or dead, or actual events is purely coincidental.

First Printing, 2022

For ordering questions, please direct your emails to authorladetwiler@gmail.com or visit www.ladetwiler.com

To my husband

"I always lock the door when I creep by daylight."

~Charlotte Perkins Gilman, "The Yellow Wallpaper"

Chapter One

Rose

Sunday

When the Taylors moved into the house at 312 Cedar Lane, the doll was already there, perched in the garage atop the heap of dusty, weathered items as if it were a goddess taking inventory of a wasteland. Rose Taylor first encountered it as she browsed the work to be done in the garage, all of the last tenant's abandoned belongings strewn about for her to deal with. She begrudgingly stared out into the front yard where her husband, Thad, directed the moving truck into the driveway, screaming at the two kids to get out of the way before they got backed over. She chilled at the thought and turned back to the tower of items.

Despite the myriad items, the doll commanded her attention above all else, inexplicably. She fought back her racing pulse at the sight of the abandoned, delicate toy. She reached out a hesitant hand to touch its pale pink dress, the dirt stains giving it an eerie, lonely vibe that enhanced the goosebumps already spreading up her arm. And in spite of its state of disarray, she smiled, knowing Lilly would love it. At five, the little girl had dozens upon dozens of dolls, but this one would probably be her favorite because it was so dirty. Rose shoved aside worries of germs and disease and cradled the doll in her weary arms, relaxing into the solid feel of its porcelain body at rest. It had been so long since a real baby had been rocked by her arms, and the memory brought both a sense of longing and a sense of peace. She closed her eyes, blocking out the beeping of the moving truck and Thad's grating voice, thinking about a time not so long ago when all was right in her world.

Or at least as right as it could be. She shoved the darkness aside, the cloud that always hovered over those early days with Lilly.

Once the truck was parked, Thad barked orders at Joshua to head inside and decide which room would be his. Lilly followed, and Rose smiled at the sight of her girl in her favorite yellow dress flouncing about. Thad walked into the garage, raising an eyebrow at Rose and the sight of the doll in her arms.

"What is *that*?" he asked her, a hint of disgust accenting his phrase. She shrugged.

"I thought Lilly might like it," she said. His face darkened slightly, and she tried to reassure herself it was fine. She was imagining it. Of course Thad loved their daughter. Still, she'd always noticed, even if only subconsciously, there was a hesitancy around the girl's name.

Perhaps he, too, was shoving aside the cloud that always was a hallmark of their union, of their daughter's birth, of all the changes it had brought about. She just hoped someday, that wouldn't be the case.

This was a fresh start, though. The town of Oakwood was just what they needed. Thad had gotten a new job working as the supervisor at the local lumber mill. It was far enough from their previous home that they could be forgotten and forget what had happened there. It would be a new start for all of them, one they desperately needed

"Let's go inside and get some things sorted out, what do you say?" he asked, ushering her inside the garage door. "We'll handle all this later."

She nodded, thinking about setting the doll down for now, but something made her stop. She didn't want to drop it there, abandon it in the filthy garage, so she carried it with her. He didn't say anything, just placing his hand on the small of her back like he so often did. They talked about moving and layout plans for the house, but neither was really listening. They never were these days.

After taking a perfunctory tour of the house, the family headed to the moving truck to begin the grueling task. She hadn't realized how much they'd accumulated over the years until they'd had to pack up their lives and move miles and miles away. The back of the truck was daunting, boxes and furniture shoved in every crevice. She wondered if the new house would ever feel like home. It probably never could, in truth. She grabbed a small box, putting the doll on top of it. She hadn't wanted to leave it behind. It was stupid, she knew, and she saw Thad eyeing her as he grabbed another box from the front.

They headed inside, Joshua also carrying a heavy box behind them. Lilly danced about, and Rose stopped to smile at her again. They set the boxes down, looking at the labels on them to decide which room they should go to. She was tired already and was about to tell Thad again that they really should have spent the money on movers. But she noticed the panicked look on his face when he opened his box, which had been unmarked. He quickly ushered it past her, heading toward the garage.

"What's in there?" she asked.

"Nothing. Old knickknacks."

But they'd been married for five years. She knew his tell when he was lying. His flushed cheeks, his darting eyes. She stepped in front of him.

"What is it?" she asked, the doll under her armpit now, hanging precariously.

"It's just some stuff that we don't need. Honestly, Rose, please, step out of the way."

There was a moment of unspoken battle as there had been so often these past six months. Joshua walked into the kitchen, standing and staring at what was becoming a common scene.

"Please," he said, but the word did little to snap her out of it. Thad and Rose stood, opposing forces on the same supposed team. She did not back down, but neither did he. His jaw clenched. She stared at him defiantly, reached out, and opened the flap.

"I told you not to," he said, pissed off now. He stormed past her. She pulled her hand back, trembling. *Deep breaths. Count to five. Focus on what you can see, hear, touch, smell.* Her therapist's words flooded her mind, but she couldn't bring herself to follow any of the advice. Thad stomped to the garage door and threw it open. Rose needed air, the walls of the place already closing in on her as if she'd lived in the house for centuries.

She blew past Joshua, who was loudly exhaling now, and shoved to the living room. She fumbled with the sliding glass door's lock for a few minutes, readjusting the doll under her armpit so as not to drop her. When she finally got it opened and stepped onto the rustic deck, filthy and peeling, she breathed in the fresh air and dropped to her knees. She fought back the waves of fear.

It's fine. It's fine. It's fine. The chant of her mornings, noons, and nights. The chant that had sewn her haggard body back together.

She rocked the doll in her arms as she stared out into the forest landscape that bordered their new home. She thought about how easy it would be to slip out into the woods and never come back. But she couldn't do that to her family. She couldn't do that to Lilly or Joshua. She had to stay strong.

Thad did not follow her. Maybe he was tired of being the rock, or maybe he was just thinking about all the boxes they still had to move. Relief flooded her at the chance for a moment of solitude. She breathed in again, standing up, and leaning on the railing to look down into her new backyard. A chill ran through her, and she clutched the doll to her tighter.

"There, there," she said, but she wasn't sure if it was for the doll or for herself. Maybe for both.

She was too focused on figuring it out to hear the words whispered into the wind, a spoken promise or curse or threat, whatever you want to call it. The words lifted up from the tree line below, the shifty eyes staring up at the woman on the deck.

If Rose Taylor had heard the phrase, she probably would have stopped Thad from unpacking any more boxes. She probably would have thrown the doll to the ground and left Oakwood, left everything behind. But she did not. She was too wrapped up in the past to sense the very imminent danger in her future.

For the words that lifted like a demented prayer in the forest covering were words that would be acted upon in five short days and ring true for two partially unsuspecting victims: "You'll fucking die."

But Rose was too distracted to sense the doom in the air—both last time, and this time, too.

Chapter Two
Rose
Monday

The house was still in disarray the next morning when Thad was preparing for work and the kids readied for school. Thad had wanted everyone to get into a new routine quickly, so when he'd arranged for the move, he hadn't given them any time at all between moving in and getting settled into school and work—except for her, of course. Because as of right now, she had no clue what sort of life or future she'd build for herself in the new town. It, like so many other things, had gone unspoken between them that she would take some time to settle in. Everyone had somewhere to be except her. She was the fragile rose to be stowed away on a shelf lest she crumble in their palms. She was sort of glad for it because if she were honest, she wasn't prepared to go out on the town and pretend this was a beautiful start for a perfect family. A big part of her wanted to stay in bed like she had for all these months and forget about everything. A huge part of her found it hard to even take the next breath. Nonetheless, looking around at the unpacked boxes everywhere, the peeling wallpaper, and the general chaos of the new home gave her anxiety all the same. Nothing felt right.

"Don't forget about your appointment today," Thad reminded her as he kissed her on the cheek. She was working on brewing coffee—the coffee pot had been deemed an essential that weekend and, thus, one of the items unpacked immediately. She nodded her head slightly, not wanting to give him the satisfaction of huffing or arguing. He'd been sure to add "find a new therapist" to his deluge of tasks for the move, a fact that only made her feel guiltier. He had lost at least twenty pounds in the past few months from the stress of it all. Add shitty wife to her repertoire these days—because she was. She didn't have the energy, though, to deal with that either.

"Josh, come on, it's time to get going," Thad yelled up the steps.

"Lilly," Rose bellowed, echoing her husband's sentiments. She'd checked on the girl, who again insisted on wearing the yellow dress for her first day of pre-school. Who was she to argue?

"Can you drop her off?" Rose asked, her eyes darting around again. They both knew why she couldn't, the unspoken words plastered on his face like a neon sign. She couldn't be trusted to drop her daughter off. The idea stung, chewing into her already ragged skin and spreading like venom through her veins.

You can't be trusted.
You're a shitty mother.
You're a shitty wife.
You've failed.

You're so weak.

You're useless.

She exhaled, knowing no amount of therapy could help her level of fucked-up these days. Still, looking at her husband, she saw a familiar although distant glow in his eyes. He cared about her. He wanted them all to be safe and happy. That was why he'd picked up their lives and abandoned a job he loved. He'd done it for her, for all of them. That was something to cling to, at least.

"Okay. Let me just make sure she has everything," Rose said after he nodded gently. Joshua stood in the kitchen, studying them both.

"Bye, buddy. Have a good day," she said. She reached in to hug him, but he pulled back. The sting in her heart intensified, but Thad put a hand on her shoulder.

"He's just going through a lot, with the move and all."

"Of course," she answered, leaving the kitchen and heading up the stairs to collect her little girl. Joshua had always been going through a lot, but now, he probably blamed this on her, too. She couldn't hold it against him, in truth. At ten, life seemed like a harrowing line of endless days out of your control. Add to that all Joshua had been through, and it was no wonder the kid was a little messed up. Perhaps they should talk to that new therapist about seeing their son, too.

That was a problem for another day, though. She ushered her family out, shouted I love yous, and returned to the quiet of the house that was now her home but felt like nothing of the sort.

She stalked around the kitchen island, her hand tracing the cool marble. The cabinets were too dark, too woody for her taste. The floor's alabaster tile was stained from age and a few splatters of what looked like red wine. The living room's green carpet reminded her of moss, and their bedroom was cold and icy. She did like the glass patio doors that extended from the living room, and she liked the open floor plan from kitchen to living room. But that was it. Glancing around at the musty, tattered house, she sighed. This was not the house of her dreams. In truth, it was no longer the life of her dreams, either. Where had the vivacious business woman who often donned the front page of newspapers and even a few magazines gone?

She headed to the sofa, needing a second to prop up her feet and take it all in. The day stretched before her, endless hours of trying to organize their old life into their new location. A gargantuan task for someone with energy and hope—a futile mission for someone like her these days. Tears welled at the prospect. When did life become such a mess? When did she become such a failure? When did she give up, and when did he give up on her?

She knew the answer, of course, but her mind shoved it back down. No use going there. Her eyes scanned the room for a distraction, and she'd found it.

The doll. It was perched on the desk in the living room, where she'd set her carefully the night before. She'd taken some time yesterday to launder the doll's soft pink dress, so now it was crisp and clean. She'd taken a washcloth and dabbed the dirt streaks from the poor thing's cheeks. Despite the crack running down its face from a previous drop or careless owner, the doll looked so real, so lifelike. If the crack weren't there, hell, Rose would even be convinced the darling thing was real.

She held the doll in her arms, thinking about what it could be like. Another baby. Another girl. She exhaled, standing up with the doll. She needed air. She needed to get away from boxes and memories, all of it. Maybe it would be good to explore the neighborhood a bit, to get out and see what possibilities were here for her.

She'd found a whole slew of doll items in the garage when she'd poked around yesterday. She walked out to the still hoarder-like garage, moving past some old lawn furniture and a broken sink that was abandoned on the floor. In the back corner, she found what she was looking for—the stroller. Dirty and dusty, but functionable. Just like her perhaps.

She tucked the doll into it. Boy, Thad and the therapist would have a field day with this one. Still, there was something about the doll, about the house, that wouldn't let her just leave it behind. Maybe it was the loneliness. Maybe it was because she'd promised Lilly to care for the doll while she was gone. They had yet to figure out a name for the little angel, but for now, Angel would suffice. She smiled, pushing the stroller into the open air and taking in the sight of the streets around her.

The woods bordered the back of the house, but from the front, it looked like a perfect little suburbia. Rows and rows of houses congruent in construction and shape lined the sidewalks. Mailboxes with numbers and bright colors lined the street, too, reminding her of their development back home. Correction. Their past home. This place was home now.

She pushed the stroller, ignoring the screeching wheel, and took in the quiet serenity of the street. There was a dog barking from somewhere, a weighty bark echoing throughout the neighborhood that startled her. She looked down at the stroller, and then laughed at her own stupidity. Had she really thought the baby would cry? That thing really would mess with your head, the lifelike features playing on her psyche apparently. She ambled onward, though, her eyes dancing over flower beds in front yards and signs with last names. She passed a white picket fence and jumped again when she saw the source of the bark. A huge black Great Dane bounced about at the fence, it's thick snout protruding over the top of its border.

"Edmund, get in here," a female voice beckoned. The dog let out another woof and then begrudgingly obeyed its owner.

Rose walked on, the squeaky wheel of the stroller resonating as she plodded forward. Her eyes took it all in, the newness admittedly exciting in a way she hadn't expected. As she rounded the corner, though, she heard a voice.

"Oh my," the woman's shrill voice announced from behind her. "Oh, God, Harold, look". Rose turned to see a couple walking on the other side of the street, just behind her. They were coming her way. When Rose shoved her red hair out of her face and smiled at them, the elderly woman gasped. The older man with her, presumably her husband, clutched her arm to keep her from falling.

"Violet, calm down. It's okay. It's not her. She's gone now, remember?" the man reassured. Rose stood stalk still, eyeing the couple as they warily ogled her. The husband gave a weak wave with his free hand and then readjusted his fedora.

"Hi! You must be the new neighbor. 312 Cedar, right?" he asked, leading his wife down the sidewalk until they were directly across from Rose and could get a better look.

"Yes, hi. Nice to meet you. I'm sorry, I didn't mean to startle you," she said, hoping to get more details on the wife's odd reaction.

"It's not a problem at all. My wife just thought you looked like someone is all."

"Like that she-devil. Oh, and you've even got that cursed doll out. What are you doing with it? Harold, what is she doing with that doll? And the red hair. It *is* her. It has to be." The wife's movements became frenetic, almost cult-like. Her arms shook, waving insanely as the husband again calmed her down.

He turned back to Rose after he'd successfully calmed his wife down to a manageable level. "I'm so sorry. Dementia," he mouthed, and Rose nodded sympathetically. Still, the hatred in the woman's eyes and the way she'd asked about the doll—it got her wondering. She wanted to ask him more questions about who lived in their house before her, but she didn't get a chance. He quickly ushered his wife back down the sidewalk the way they had already traveled, turning her attention to ice cream and Frank Sinatra. That seemed to work, for the lady started laughing and smiling, almost as if a switch had flipped.

Rose calmed her breathing and walked on, the tire of the stroller now putting her on edge. Her heart beat wildly as if it would combust at any second. Something about the encounter didn't feel right. Something about the way the woman had stared at her, how she'd mentioned her hair and the doll. Rose looked down at the being, resting in the stroller, as the question rolled in her head.

What had happened at 312 Cedar before they'd gotten there?

She did a U-turn with the stroller and headed back to the mysterious house, knowing the answers, if there were anywhere, wouldn't be on the picturesque, silent street. As she walked past the picket fence again, the big dog let out a single howl from inside the window as if to tell her to turn back.

Chapter Three
The Watcher
Monday

The misty morning cloaked her in the veil of the trees. She squinted to get a better look as the bitch returned with the stroller. Shit. She'd lost her chance now.

She'd watched the redhead leave her new house a little while after the rest of the family. Pushing the stroller down the sidewalk, the Watcher hoped she would get a chance to do some snooping and see if there was anything of use. Not that she needed to, of course. She'd been prepared for this. She'd done her homework, and she knew the layout of the house. She had everything memorized—every nook, every cranny, every loose board. It would be of help to her when the time came, she knew. She'd taken her time because that's who the Watcher was—prepared. A perfectionist. A force to be reckoned with, even if they failed to believe it. Sometimes, it helped to be underestimated.

In truth, she could just end it all today, right here. She probably should. She could get her revenge and move on with

19

her glorious plan. She could take what was rightfully and calm her breaking heart. She thought about how quickly she could end the fucking saga. It was tempting. Nevertheless, she didn't move. She stood in the tree line, watching and waiting. She had some other stars to align, some other loose ends to meticulously sort. She wouldn't mess this up. Too many like her were in a rush and fucked up. But not her. She was smart, cunning, and most of all, patient. Hadn't she proven that already?

She'd been so patient already. Not that she'd had a choice.

She watched the redhead shove the stroller through the front door. A few moments later, the woman again emerged on the deck, standing out and looking into the trees. Her eyes darted about as if she sensed the Watcher's presence lurking below. She shook her head. Quiet desperation. That's what that one reeked of. She would laugh if it wasn't so sad. So many people had intuition if they just took the time to listen to it. Just to be safe, though, the Watcher tucked herself behind the tree, stretching her neck and looking up at the forested sky. Her clothes were damp from sleeping out under the stars the past couple of nights. Her neck ached from the lack of support on the floor of the van. It was worth it, though. It would all be worth it. Soon.

She peeked out once more. The redhead leaned over the railing now, taking in the sights, breathing in deeply as if she had to calm her nerves. That pissed the Watcher off. After all that had happened. After all she had personally lost, all that had driven her here, now, fighting for what was hers. She would reclaim what was hers, though. If it killed her. The bitch wouldn't move in on her territory without paying.

She had to stifle a laugh. Of course it wouldn't kill her, the Watcher. It would kill the one being watched, when she least expected it. A mother, after all, will go to any lengths for a child.

She should know that by fucking now. She should fucking know that, sitting in her picture-perfect life.

Chapter Four

Rose

Monday

She went to make herself a cup of coffee but realized they were all out of grounds. She sighed, adding the grocery store to her list of errands. Glancing around the house at all the boxes, she pulled her hair back into a ponytail and decided to get a few unpacked before heading out again. She put on her playlist and got to work, thinking about the days when this playlist was in the background of her salon and not some dingy new house in the middle of a new, foreign land.

She started in the kitchen, unpacking forks, juicers, and relics of wedding gifts they'd received so many years ago. An extra toaster they'd never used yet, an extra set of serving ware. Into cupboards and drawers it all poured, the hopes and dreams of a couple who were much more naïve then. A couple who thought the world would be perfect as long as they lived on love.

The next hour or so ticked by in domestic monotony. It had been six months since she'd had somewhere to be outside of the domestic bubble and, in truth, most days she missed it. Her work clothes sat untouched in boxes, her sweatpants and favorite graphic t-shirts her uniform now. She wondered how the new owner of her shop was doing. Did she keep the décor the same? Had she changed the name yet? And what about all her beloved clients? Had they mourned the loss of her or, like everything else in her life, said goodbye quickly and moved to the next thing?

The sobering thought made her plop on the stool at the island. She had complained about how the last tenant had left so many of their personal belongings and furniture behind, but she was glad for the bar stool now. She leaned on her hands, trying to remind herself it was for the best. Still, it had been hard leaving behind the thing of her dreams, the thing she'd worked so hard for once upon a time.

Glitz and Glam Salon had been her dream since she was ten—and with Thad, the dream had come true. She'd worked her way up to not just being a hometown stylist, but a stylist worthy of envy. She'd done hair for professional shoots, for celebrities, for the local higher-end clients. She'd earned her reputation as coloring queen and updo royalty. She'd devoted her life to her craft.

And now, with the flick of a wrist, it was gone.

He'd told her she could start a new salon in Oakwood. "You did it once," he said. "You could do it again. It might be fun to redesign your business from the ground up."

But he didn't get it. He really didn't. He was too worried about painting on the fake fucking smile and getting back to his career to notice the truth—she didn't want to start over.

She wanted her old life back, cracks and all. She wanted the past, something she could never have again.

Didn't he?

That was an improvement, she realized as she slowly picked herself off the stool and returned to the box she'd been working on. For a long while after the situation, she hadn't wanted anything at all. She hadn't wanted to breathe let alone work. She hadn't wanted to wash her own hair let alone mastermind new looks for others. She wanted to fade into oblivion in a black hole, to fall deep into a well that no one could throw a long enough rope down. She was eviscerated, body and soul, and she didn't want to emerge from her carefully constructed cocoon of depression.

But he'd made her. He'd convinced her it was best for the kids. She owed them that, he had said. It wasn't good for them to be surrounded by the past, he'd told her. She could see the truth now, though. He didn't want to live with a tarnished image. Mr. Fucking Perfect wanted to stay that way—and he'd go to the ends of the earth if he had to in order to start anew.

They were different that way. She concerned herself with knowing what really was—he with protecting what he thought could be. Two different souls, one marriage, two houses, and a past that loomed too close for comfort.

She put the spoons away and the spatulas. She studied the coffee pot, her head pounding. She hadn't slept well the past few nights, worse than usual. Every noise, every bump, every squeak had sent her into a panic. She really needed to finish unpacking, and the kids would be home in a few hours. Still, she didn't think her weary bones could handle keeping her upright for one more minute if she didn't get some coffee in her blood. Some real coffee complete with the café experience, the soft music, the choices etched on a charming chalkboard. So, she used her phone to google what coffee places were in the area. She was thrilled to see there was one only about five blocks away. She thought about taking the doll with her again but then decided against it.

It was a fresh start, after all. She didn't need the town talking about her as if she were crazy already, did she? Still as she gathered her keys and looked at the doll perched in her stroller by the door, a pang of sudden regret hit her. It felt odd leaving her here.

"Sorry, Lilly," she said, her voice scratchy from not using it. And she was. A promise was a promise, after all.

A promise was a fucking promise.

MAYBE IT WAS THE DÉCOR or maybe it was because the barista seemed as equally lonely as she was, but Rose couldn't bring herself to get the cup of coffee and quickly leave Rachel's Brews like she should. She lingered a while at the counter, inhaling the solace from the smell of the earthy, dark scent. Soft music played in the background as the barista, Millie, swiped a rag across the counter and chatted to Rose brightly about the weather, the town, and the latest gossip. She acted like Rose had lived in Oakwood her whole life, even though she had told the girl she'd just moved in. Millie had nodded, though, as if she already knew that. She probably did. Oakwood was the proverbial small town where everyone knew everything about all the others, and outsiders were perused with wary eyes.

All of the tables were empty in the coffee shop except for a corner booth where an elderly woman tapped on the glass at a single robin. Serenity intermingled with a sense of belonging there, and Rose exhaled for the first time in days.

"Stay for a while?" Millie asked, gesturing toward a tiny table near the counter. "The soap operas are just getting ready to start. You won't want to miss that."

Rose smiled. "I really should get back. I have a lot of unpacking to do."

"Hey, suit yourself, but if it were me, I'd be taking advantage of the peace and my coffee. Besides, I like talking to you. There's a good aura about you."

Flattered, Rose claimed a seat, setting her coffee on the shiny top of the table. "Really? You can tell that already?"

"You can tell a lot by a person's eyes and smile. You're a gentle soul, Rose. You'll fit in this town perfectly, I think."

"Thanks," she said as she glanced up at the television mounted in the corner. The elderly woman tapping on the glass spun around to get a better look. She even clapped slightly, enthralled by the opening music.

"Can you turn it up, Dearie?" she shouted from across the room, and Millie obliged.

It did feel good to sit down, Rose decided. It felt good to just be a woman in the coffee shop, taking in the atmosphere. She glanced around at the neon-colored walls, the abstract paintings. Something in her awakened, something that had died—well, when it had all happened. She sipped on her coffee, the liquid scalding her tongue, but she didn't care. She needed to jolt her mind back to the present. Pain has a purpose, sometimes. Pain wasn't always bad, she'd come to learn. Physical pain, at least.

"So, what house is it you moved into?" Millie asked during the commercial break.

Rose turned to eye the girl. "312 Cedar."

Millie didn't move her eyes from her. "Really?" she asked, a look of disdain painting itself on her face.

A chill reverberated through Rose. What the hell had happened there? First, there had been the woman on the walk, and now, Millie clearly startled at the mention of the address.

"Who lived there before me?" Rose asked.

Millie looked over at the woman in the corner and then eyed the door, as if to make sure no one was listening. The elderly woman was still staring intently at the television so as to not miss a second of the stories when they popped back on.

"We don't talk about it." Mille's words were a whisper, yet they filled the room with their bold claim, their harsh tone.

Rose tilted her head, slowly panning her eyes around the room as if she were missing something. She returned her attention to Millie, who was paler now, but trying to cover her emotions with an off-tune whistle of a familiar song. It only underscored the chill in the air.

"What do you mean?" Rose ventured.

"I mean we don't talk about it. I've said too much already," Millie snapped, staring directly at Rose as if she could see into the inner layer of her soul. Rose didn't feel welcome anymore.

"You can't just—"

"Enough!" the elderly lady in the corner of the room shouted, covering her ears with her hands. She rocked herself in the booth, her head hitting against the wooden back so hard, each crack stopped Rose's heart just a little. She peered in horror, expecting to see blood gushing down from her tightly curled head. Millie crossed the café and tried to calm Mrs. Heathrow, as Rose discovered her name was.

"We don't talk about it," Millie shouted again over her shoulder, and Rose quickly got up, grabbed her coffee, and left the café.

She stood for a long moment in front of the shop, staring into the desolate street. A few fallen leaves scattered as she stepped forward, readjusting a strand of hair that had fallen from her ponytail. She breathed in the cold air as a bird cawed in the distance. A lone car travelled down the street. She felt the desolation deep within as she studied the dreary town hiding behind the façade of charm. What the hell was going on? The town was giving her definite vibes that something was amiss. She felt suddenly like they'd walked into a horror movie and she was the only one who didn't know the killer.

Had someone been murdered in their house? Had someone done something awful? Could it be haunted? She needed to talk to Thad. Certainly, the realtor would have revealed any details like that for fear of a lawsuit if it wasn't disclosed, right? Still, the encounters she'd had with the townsfolk today didn't instill confidence. There was a definite "us versus them" mentality when it came to newcomers—and the Taylors, as she found out, were definitely being watched as just that. The townsfolk didn't trust them, which wasn't alarming in itself. What was truly frightening was the question: What exactly were they trying to protect?

We don't talk about it.

We don't talk about it.

The words echoed in her head as she jogged home, peering over her shoulder every block to make sure she was truly alone.

As her feet pounded on the pavement, though, Rose considered the conversation at the café. There was one problem with Millie's words. If she said they didn't talk about it, it was almost certain that someone, in fact did. And Rose knew exactly where to go to get the town's truest, juiciest gossip, outsider or not.

Chapter Five

Rose

Monday Night

She set the table, pretending to be the domestic goddess she didn't feel like anymore—and in truth, wasn't. The chicken nuggets and fries she'd thrown in the oven were overly crispy, and she couldn't even find the plates so she'd set the table with paper towels and flatware. It would have to do. She stared at the four empty spots at the table. Things had been rocky, and the food certainly wasn't great. Still, at least they would have dinner together.

Thad came home on time, which was exciting, the kids in tow. Maybe things would be different here, she thought as she smiled at the kids. She wrapped her arms around Lilly. Joshua brushed by her, and she shot Thad a look. He didn't say anything, and she felt resentment rise.

The doll sat on the fifth chair beside Lilly. Rose had taken care of the doll, had done her motherly duty. She was exhausted from the day's events but also energized by the prospect of figuring some things out tomorrow.

"How was work?" she asked Thad as they sat down to the tray of overly browned chicken nuggets and fries. She carefully scooped out servings onto the paper towels, awaiting a snide remark from someone. Everyone seemed too tired to criticize her, though.

"Busy but good. I think I'm going to like it there," Thad said, and proceeded to chat about names she didn't know and terms she never understood. Still, she smiled, happy to see her husband energized. It wasn't hard for him, though. Work made him happy, and he'd always been good at supervising. He'd climbed the ladder back home to the top of his field, and so when the opening at Oakwood popped up on his job search, she knew undoubtedly the lumber mill in town would scoop him up. They'd be foolish not to with his experience.

"I'm glad it's going well for you," she said, trying not to stall and highlight the unspoken finish to the sentence—that at least someone's career was blossoming. She was lucky, she knew, that her husband's salary was enough to support them so work for her was a luxury. Still, it was a hard pill to swallow. She'd always prided herself on her work, too. She wondered if she'd ever feel like that again.

One day at a time, she reminded herself. *One day at a time. Focus on the task at hand.* And that task, right now, was sorting out what the hell had happened in the house.

"What did you do today?" Thad asked, turning the conversation to her as he served himself some extra chicken nuggets.

She thought about telling him, her mouth opening to reveal the creepy vibes she had about the house. She thought about discussing her plans for the next day to sort through it all. Something, though, stopped her. She looked at the man across the table, the successful man who always had it together. And suddenly, she felt unworthy, less than. He was working his way up the field already on his first day, and she was... what? Playing detective about something that probably didn't even matter?

"Oh, you know. Ran a few errands. Went to the coffee shop," she said. "How about you, Joshua? How was school?"

"Fine," he said, and then stood up from the table. She went to tell him to sit back down, but Thad threw out a hand to stop her.

"I've got homework," the boy said, not bothering to push in his chair or look back at them.

She felt her lip quivering, but Thad shook his head. "It's fine. He's at that stage, and he's struggling with the move. He'll come around."

She couldn't say it, but she wanted to tell Thad he'd never come around, not really. Sure, in the early days of their relationship when she showered him with gifts and tried to be the cool stepmom, he was okay. But when things got serious and suddenly, she was pregnant with Lilly, things changed completely.

Part of it was probably animosity towards her, an outsider. Part of it was probably his mother's poisonous comments about her. Part of it was just that they were so different.

Lilly kept nibbling on her chicken nuggets, and Rose smiled down at her. She wasn't supposed to play favorites, she knew. But how could she not when their sweet girl was—well, so sweet? When she first met Thad, she didn't know if she could be a mom. Joshua seemed to confirm her fears. But when

Lilly came along, she realized motherhood was her calling, her passion, and her purpose. Joshua had made her a mother by default, but Lilly had made her realize her true happiness in the role. How could she not dote on her more?

"Listen, I'll help you clean up, and then I have to go back to the office," Thad said. Rose paused.

"What?" This wasn't what she'd pictured. She'd thought this new town would mean more time together, less loneliness. She thought they would set up their new home together. She'd pictured all the greeting card, holiday movie, warm moments already. This was not part of the picture.

"There's a dinner tonight, and the owners want me to come as a sort of introduction to the community. A lot of our clients are invited."

"I see," she said.

She stood up and busied her hands, trying not to let the rejection sink in.

"Hey, hey, look at me," he said, pulling her into him and wrapping her in his arms. She set down the tray of now cold chicken nuggets. "I didn't mean to upset you. I just didn't think you'd want to come with me, and we don't really know any babysitters here."

He spun her in his arms, and she looked up at his perfect jawline, the eyes that had sucked her in. The lies flowed so effortlessly off his tongue. His steady voice, deep and comforting, could convince anyone of anything.

But not her. She knew the truth. It wasn't about what was best for her or the kids. It was that he was embarrassed by her. He didn't trust her anymore, and he was worried about his reputation. She was a danger to his image. This fresh start was about him, not about them, she uncovered with certainty. Frustration building, she shrugged out of his arms.

"I don't want to put pressure on you," he added, a white flag on the battlefield between them. She shot her gun at it.

"Whatever you say," she replied and turned an icy back to him. He exhaled. She had won, but what good was a claim to victory if it left her alone, abandoned, and lost?

He hated silence between them. It was her greatest weapon. Lately, though, nothing but silence echoed through them, between them, enveloping their relationship in a shell.

In their new bedroom with the door shut, she stared out into the dark forest behind their humble abode. A tree branch shook even though there was no wind. A chill shook through her, and she backed away from the window. She'd always hated windows as a little girl, afraid the boogie monster or a yeti would appear. Now, all she could see was her haggard reflection and an empty forest, a reminder of what would never be again.

Chapter Five
Rose
Tuesday

The salon in Oakwood sat about four stores down from the coffee shop she'd been to the day before. She skipped over the coffee shop, chilling at the thought of Millie's ominous words. She'd walked down without the stroller this time, but she'd put the doll in her tote bag that Thad always said was too big. Maybe he was right, since a human-sized baby fit in there with ease. She knew it was ridiculous when she packed the doll into her bag. Still, she felt bad leaving it at the house alone while Lilly was gone. She'd told her she'd watch the doll again, and she would. She couldn't bear the thought of something happening to it while she was out.

The doors to the salon rang as she entered, her gaze landing on the sign announcing "walk-ins welcome." In truth, that probably meant either the salon wasn't very good or there just weren't too many salon-visiting residents in town, because back home at her salon, she never had room in her schedule for walk-ins. That didn't matter, though, she told her overly critical mind.

"Can I help you?" a woman with a deep Southern drawl asked, her lips heavily outlined in neon pink liner and filled in with a pink two shades too light. Her vivacious smile, though, warmed her face and made you forget about the inexpertly drawn lips.

"I was hoping to get a cut and color," Rose announced. She could easily touch up her hair herself, but she wasn't really here to improve her looks. She was here for one thing, the best thing you could get a at any salon—gossip. If she were to crack the code about what happened to the woman in her house, this was the starting point. This was the place where all of the town's juicy gossip would be centered. She just had to be careful and not seem too eager.

"Angelica, do you have time, honey?" she asked. A girl with jet-black, wavy hair that was down the middle of her back peeked from around a mirror.

"Yep, just finishing up a style." She smiled, and Rose offered a little wave before plopping down in a chair in the waiting area.

The salon was charming in a quaint, farmhouse sort of way. Little distressed wood stands held sunflower bouquets, and there were farmhouse pictures everywhere. It was the kind of salon you'd expect to find in a small town like Oakwood.

When it was her turn a few minutes later, she let Angelica lead her to her chair. She eyed the products and the tools she had at her station, unable to stop herself from passing silent judgement on the girl's skill. These days, it wasn't like Rose had somewhere to be or someone to impress. If Angelica messed her hair up too badly, she could always fix it—and it didn't matter anyway. It was a small price to pay to get the answers she needed.

She set her bag on the stand, hoping now that it didn't splay open and reveal the unorthodox contents of her bag. She needed to ease into the conversation, and warming up to Angelica would not be as simple if she thought she was crazy.

"So, new in town, huh?" Angelica asked after they discussed a plan for her hair.

"Yes, we just got here this weekend. My husband was offered a new job."

"Where at?" Angelica asked, snipping at her locks. Rose hated when hairstylists tried to use this trendy technique to cut hair. There was a much simpler way to handle it.

"J. B. Lumber. He's a supervisor there."

"Oh, that's a good place. My father-in-law is friends with them. So, are you liking it in town?"

Snip, snip. Tell a few lies. Snip, snip. Tell a few more. Get her right where you want her, Rose thought.

Rose told Angelica all the right things. She lied about her old job, not wanting to answer questions about why a former salon owner would be here now—she went with librarian. She'd always liked books, so it wasn't too much of a stretch. She mentioned her kids and how she loved cats and might get one now that they were settled. She asked questions, too, peppering in inquisitions that seemed harmless and raving about the show Angelica said she loved.

"Oh, 312 Cedar? That's not too far from here," Angelica replied when they got onto the subject of where Rose lived. She'd stopped the haircut, staring appraisingly into the mirror at Rose. A quiet tension filled the air at the mention of the address, though. It was a blip across the stylist's face, but Rose was attuned to it. She smiled gently so as not to draw attention to it and continue driving the conversation where she needed it to go.

"Yeah, so far, it's a pretty nice place. I can't complain. Other than the fact the tenant left some things behind. A whole lot of stuff. Do you know who it was that lived there? I haven't gotten around to asking my husband about it with the move and all." Rose picked at a fingernail nonchalantly, reminding herself to stay calm, to lie well. That was never a problem for her, in truth, though. She'd been lying for months, the fake smile plastered on her face in public when it needed to be. The "I'm fine" lie had become the biggest in her toolkit, sprouting confidence in her to expand her lies to bigger, greater things.

Angelica clammed up, tension all over her face. She glanced around the shop. The receptionist was on the phone. She leaned in close to Rose, the scissors near her cheek. Rose's heart stopped, the sharp shears almost grazing her skin.

"We don't like to talk about it," she whispered, her words ragged and staccato.

"Oh, it's just there's so much left. I thought they might want it back."

She stared into Rose's eyes through the mirror. "I said we don't like to talk about it." Her words were firm but paradoxically gentle, too. Rose felt entranced by her hazel eyes lasering into hers.

"I'm sorry. I just—if you could give me a name, I would love to see if they want some of it back."

Angelica glanced back to the desk and looked over her other shoulder. "I shouldn't tell you this," she finally whispered. Her words were harsh and menacing. She turned back, glowering at Rose as if her glare could will her into submissive silence. She continued, "but the Denvilles used to own that place. A good, hardworking family. When Mr. Denville died, his widow was left behind. She eventually got too sick last year to care for the place, poor thing. When she went to a nursing home, the family decided they would rent it out for a while until they sorted affairs out. A newcomer in town moved in for a while." The words spewed from Angelica's lips, the shears too close for comfort still. But Rose listened intently, not wanting to miss a single word. She could not have overlooked the angrily barked word "newcomer" even if she wanted to. It was clear that Rose was correct in her assumption: Oakwood was a closed-off community. As if the word reminded Angelica of the fact she was dealing with another newcomer, she pulled back slightly and cleared her throat, glancing again at the receptionist.

"So what happened?" Rose pushed, not ready to let go of it all so quickly.

Angelica exhaled. She bit her lip. Rose stared at her through the mirror, not wanting to look desperate but desperate nevertheless.

"There was a situation. An incident. And then she was just gone. Left all of her things, from what I've heard. Left town. It wasn't long before you got here. A few months maybe. The family was dealing with Ms. Denville's death by that time and just didn't have the energy left to clean out the place, I guess. Which is probably why you inherited so much. Hopefully at least there were some valuables in there." Angelica set down her sheers, fluffing Rose's hair.

"I'm going to go mix your dye now," she said.

Rose thought about biting her lip, but the receptionist was still on the phone and the shop was empty other than her. This was her chance.

"What was her name? The lady who lived there? It's just, I have so much sentimental stuff left over from her, and I'd love to track her down."

Angelica put herself in front of Rose, now looking straight into her eyes.

"I wouldn't go hunting for her. That one was a lunatic, let's just say that. Dangerous even. Her name was Cloey Fountain. A redhead like you. Probably why the town's been so edgy. It's just sort of creepy, you know? Two redheads in the same house, both outsiders. No offense."

"Oh, none taken," Rose said, smiling her own perfect grin.

"I'll be right back," Angelica replied, spinning Rose in her chair a bit.

Rose felt like leaving the salon. She'd gotten what she wanted. Still, it was better to play it safe. She had the name now. She just had to do some more digging. She told herself to hold back the smile that was forming. She felt like she'd accomplished something grand, a feeling now foreign to her.

While she waited for Angelica to return, she watched the receptionist work for a while, the big, pink grin on her face looking almost too big too be real now. At any moment, her face would crack, Rose was certain. Like the porcelain doll in her bag, she would crack and splinter from the pressure of it all.

Everything did in time.

Cloey Fountain.

What had she done? And where was she now?

Rose wanted to rock the doll, to feel its weight in her arms, but she knew there would be time for that.

DESPITE HER CONDESCENDING inner monologue about Angelica's work, Rose had to admit that it looked pretty good. Not perfect, but good, and, in reality, way better than it had looked in months. She decided after finishing up at the salon she would take the bus and visit Thad at work for lunch under the ruse of showing off her new hair. He would be glad to see she was making an effort again. Maybe he'd even think she was okay now. Maybe he'd drop his guard and give her the information she was after—if he knew what had happened to the tenant before them.

She doubted it. Still, if he did know, he probably had guarded the truth. By the sounds of it, Cloey had been involved in some sort of a scandal and, if it was of a delicate nature, Thad wouldn't risk upsetting her. Always the armor, shielding her from life's shittiest moments.

Except where had he been when it had happened? When it all went down? The questions creeped into her battered brain, but she squashed them as quickly as they appeared. It was fine. It was all fine now. Her family was together. Her kids, Thad—that was the only thing that mattered now.

She walked to the front desk of the J.B. Lumber offices and saw a chipper brunette smiling too wide behind the desk. After exchanging pleasantries so fake her face felt like it would crack in half, Evette was ushered to her husband's new office. She looked around at the fluorescent, too-bright walls and wondered if he was already loved here. Probably. He was like that—loved everywhere, no matter what he did. Darkness didn't permeate him in the way it did her, and the past didn't mar him indelibly. He rose above it, at all costs.

"Hey, Honey, I didn't expect to see you here," he said as she plopped a brown paper bag on his desk. She thought he looked uncomfortable, shoving his hands into his pockets as if to still them. Perhaps he hadn't wanted to reveal this dragon behind the curtain yet, his wife who had been quieted in the night by a move to a new town. Perhaps here, at this office, there was still a chance he could convince them his wife was normal, good. Perhaps.

"I just wanted to bring you lunch, see how you were doing. Your office is nice," she said, smiling as she glanced around. She ambled behind his desk, her hands tracing the smooth, wooden top. She noticed there were no pictures of the family yet. He had just started. *Give him a break.* But maybe—

"So thoughtful. How is the unpacking coming along? Did you do any exploring?"

She shrugged, turning to face the man who knew her intimately yet no longer knew her at all, it sometimes seemed. He perused her now, as if on cue. "Love the new hair," he said, smiling too big. "Did you do it?"

"Of course not. My blending is way better than this," she replied, grinning in spite of the predicament. "I decided to treat myself, check out the salon in town."

"So did you get some gossip then?" he asked, showing off his knowledge of salon life after being married to a stylist for so long.

"Yes. I actually wanted to talk to you about it," she said as he opened up the paper sack and pulled out the foil-wrapped, greasy sandwich. He glanced at her now, interest piqued.

"The girls at the salon were sort of acting strange about the woman who lived in our house before us. I guess her name was Cloey Fountain. Did you hear anything about her? Like, did the owners who sold the house to us say anything? The realtor?"

He shrugged. "No, not really. It was kind of a quick deal. They were in a hurry. I mean, the realtor warned me that the last tenant left in a hurry and left a bunch of stuff, but she said the owner would have it moved to the garage at the very least. So I didn't really ask. Why?"

She wrapped her arms around her, eyeing him to see if he had any of his tells. He did not. If she had to guess, she thought he was telling the truth. She didn't know if she should be relieved or irritated because now, her hunt for the truth was even more difficult.

"Probably just had to leave town for an emergency or something," he said. "We left in a hurry, after all."

She nodded, thoughts swirling of their old town, their old life. He seemed to sense the emotions he'd conjured with his words because regret painted itself on his clean-shaven face.

"Look, let's not worry about it, okay? The thing is, we got this nice house. We've got a chance to start over. Let's not some mystery lady ruin this for us, okay?"

Everything is ruined, she longed to whisper, but she could no longer show him her whole truth. So, she did what she'd gotten used to. She nodded and plastered on the weak smile that made him feel like it was okay. Just like he liked. Just like he wanted.

He kissed her on the cheek, and she said goodbye, returning to the odd, contorted life that was hers but didn't feel like it.

Chapter Six
The Watcher
Tuesday

Looking out at the forest sanctuary, gloomy and foreboding but welcoming in its own right, she was thankful that Oakwood had been the settling point. At least if she were to keep watch, she was in a place of peace. She'd always loved the woods, her happiest memories existing in the space between the trees, the water, the grass. She breathed in the deep air and closed her eyes. So much had gone down in her life. So, so much. But it wasn't done yet.

The Watcher sat in her peeling, white van, the door wide open. She sipped her water as she sat cross-legged on the stained fabric seats. She'd bought the van off of some creepy guy for $1,000. It had taken up a lot of her savings, but she didn't care. She needed something to be her home base, and the tent from the sporting goods store wasn't cutting it on the chilly fall nights. She had planned ahead, had done her homework. For after it was done, she would need a way to transport the body. Or bodies. She hadn't decided yet. Probably just body. But you never knew once the urge struck.

The forest cloaked the van in a forcefield of darkness. Lucky for her, the town rarely ventured this deep into the woods—too busy with their suburbia lives of lattes, school, and office jobs. The rest were too afraid of what lurked in the forest. She'd read about the legends, after all. Every town has its secrets.

This town's secrets were downright foolish. Nonetheless, it was a good town if you wanted to disappear. Small, quiet, and creepy. Full of hidden legends and the missing. She slipped in under the cover of night, planted her van, and waited. Oh, she was good at waiting, she'd learned these past few months.

She would give anything to have a hot coffee, but the prospect was too risky. If she started wandering into town now, people would notice. She'd changed her hair up, but that was no guarantee. She had to be so damn careful. The nosy gossips of the town took note of every freaking thing in a place like this. Outsiders were treated warily, as she'd learned quickly. Plus, she had a reputation to think about. Even changing her hair color wouldn't be enough. They would talk, and if they started talking, her plan would be ruined.

A bird cawed in the distance. She should be getting back to her post, but she couldn't help but feel like she had time. Rose was always one to skirt work. There was no way she'd stay in the house all day unpacking when there were coffees to be bought, nails to be done, and other general procrastinating tasks at hand. The woman called herself a mother. She didn't deserve the title. The Watcher's blood boiled at the thought.

She didn't deserve any of it. She didn't.

Not that the Watcher wanted to know married life again. She'd done that and had found it to be—well, suffocating. Exhausting. Unhinged.

She'd taken care of that part of her life. She'd found herself in the single life. Still, motherhood was her greatest calling, and this bitch was getting in the way of that. She had to pay. No one took her child and lived to tell about it. No one.

She could've looked past some of the transgressions. She could've kept her mouth shut. She'd promised herself she wouldn't partake in any more of that dark shit. But her fingers were itchy again. She missed the feel of the knife in her hands. She missed the color of blood spilling out.

She went to the duffel bag she had stowed under the passenger seat. She rooted around until she found the one she needed. Sharp. Sturdy. Foreboding. The harbinger of death nestled in her hands deliciously. She traced the blade with her fingernails, thinking about how soon, so soon, it would meet its final flesh on the other end. The sharpness of the blade sliding against her nail sent shivers down her spine. She closed her eyes and imagined that sensuous, warm feeling of the blade ripping into supple flesh.

Her flesh.

She forced herself to open her eyes and focus. First, there was playing to be done. She could not make it easy, could not send the lunatic into the good night so quietly, so gently. She deserved worse than the quick, efficient death from a blade right away. Besides, as she'd come to learn, the build-up was half the fun. She'd been too quick before.

It wouldn't be hard to make her pay. The Watcher could see it in the way she looked out into the forest, in her uncertain steps, in the way she peered over her shoulder all the time. Rose was already one step away from crazy. Admittedly, the Watcher knew the feeling all too well. She could discern its presence in another even if they couldn't. Her heart ached a little at the realization, but then she ran a hand through her hair.

"Get a grip," she told herself. "There's work to be done."

Work always made her feel better. Purpose made her feel better. And her purpose now was two-fold: Claim the child and make the fucking wench pay for her sins. She would have to pay.

The Watcher took the knife and sliced her hand, just like he had sliced her heart. Just like she had sliced at her heart, she reminded herself. It wasn't actually his fault. He was doing his best, which for men, didn't mean much. But women—women knew better. They should know better than to do what Rose did. The Watcher felt the sting of pain in her palm and looked down to see the red spreading on her alabaster skin. It was sticky and warm, off-putting in a sense. But she smiled, watching the patterns play out in dazzling red as the biting sensation reminded her—she was alive. She was still alive.

She closed her eyes and thought of the feel of the baby in her arms. She missed that full, tender feeling, that purpose, that meaning. That was what really made her feel alive. This was a weak substitute, in truth. It felt like centuries ago she'd felt that warm body cradled in her arms. How long had it been? She couldn't get that back, not completely, she admitted. She wasn't crazy, after all. She knew some feelings, some moments were fleeting. She understood some things were long gone for her.

Still, she could get some of it back. She could try. And, at the very least, she could make the bitch suffer. There was comfort in that, at least.

When the Watcher opened her eyes and brought herself back to the forest clearing and her next mission, a smile spread on her face. She had a new goal now, one she would not only succeed at, but would fucking reach glory with. She'd had a taste for blood in the past. He knew that. Or at least he found that out the hard way. Now, though, she didn't need him. She just needed her. Her and her fucking sad, begging eyes, imploring her for forgiveness.

There would be justice, and in that bloody justice, there would be a malevolent peace.

Bitches didn't deserve a quick end, after all.

The Watcher shut the van door, cracked her fingers, and headed to the front of the house to resume her post and carry out the next step of Rose's unraveling.

Chapter Seven
Rose
Tuesday

In the glimmer of the sun, the red streaks resembled a clay-laden mud, but as Rose walked closer to the door, her eyes settled on the biting truth. Blood. The words were written in blood on the porcelain-white door, dripping but blatantly legible.

You'll pay.

A simple phrase splattered in—no, it couldn't be, her might tried to deflect—but yes, yes it was— blood. It was undoubtedly blood that smeared her door with the ominous warning. A scream settled in her bones but would not escape from her open mouth as fear paralyzed her. Her throat threatened to close as she choked on the scream, on the words, on the truth. Questions of who and why and how resonated through her simultaneously, sending her blood to an icy temperature she recognized.

She backed up from the door, inching away hurriedly. She glanced behind her as if the suspect would be waiting for her.

Maybe they were. Maybe this was just the beginning and her house would become one of horrors. They were new in town. How could someone already have a vendetta against them? Her mind raced with trauma. Old memories suffocated her.

A twig snapped to the right of the house, and her heart jolted. Her head spun toward the sound as she braced herself. Her eyes scanned wildly, but they landed on nothing out of the ordinary. She thought about jumping in her car in the driveway, but her legs were heavy anchors cemented to the pavement as she stared at the house once more. Her gaze again traced the words, following each meticulous curve of every letter. Finally, she told herself to act. She pawed through her pocket as she backed up from the door, getting out her phone to call Thad or 911. Or maybe she should dash to a neighbor's house. She didn't even know them or if they were home. Her hands shook with the phone in her hand. *Phone. Police. Thad. Car. Get Away. Danger.*

She was wasting precious minutes. She needed to sort it out and quickly. Finally, the fog of indecision wafted away, and she found her legs carrying her down the street. She hunkered near a neighbor's shed, got out her phone, and dialed the three digits that would hopefully make it all go away. Her breathing labored, every inhale insanely painful, she spewed out the description of her problem and stammered her way through the unfamiliar address. She waited until she heard the sirens, then braved up enough to peek out around the shed and head toward the scene of the crime as she called Thad.

"IT'S ALL CLEAR. YOU can come inside now," the officer barked to Thad and Rose after an eternity of waiting had crawled by. Thad had wrapped his arm around her as she shivered, mostly from the bitter rattling of fear within.

Thad led her into the house, which felt like she was walking into a haunted asylum at this point. The already cold, stark walls seemed to taunt her with possibilities.

You'll pay. You'll pay. You'll pay. The bloodstained phrase wormed its way through every fiber of her being and lurked behind every corner.

"Everything checked out. No sign of entry into the house," the officer said, flipping open his notepad to ask more questions now that the immediate danger was neutralized.

He asked them questions, but Rose barely heard. She saw the doll perched on the counter. Odd. She didn't remember leaving it there. She looked to the officer, thought about mentioning it. Something in his grim face, his stoic mustache, told her not to bring it up. She didn't want him to think the town crazy had moved in.

She answered questions about time and place, details about everything to the point that she felt as if she were being interrogated. Inside her overwrought brain, she pondered the idea that maybe she was being considered as a suspect. The thought made her stomach churn.

"Listen, Mr. and Mrs. Taylor, I wouldn't worry too much. It's probably just some punk teenagers in town playing a trick. You know how kids are, and, well, Oakwood kind of likes to keep to itself."

He stared at them, and Rose felt her skin prickle. Why was the whole town hellbent on keeping everyone out? They'd barely been here a few days, and already, their status as other was being slammed into their face again and again. Moving here was clearly a mistake, she thought. They would never belong here. The town would apparently see to it.

But Thad didn't seem to think so. He shook the officer's hand, thanking him profusely. The two started some garbage conversation about sports teams and the diner in town. The officer mentioned in passing he would check the neighbor's cameras to see if they caught anything suspicious but that most didn't have those fancy contraptions in this area. There was no need, after all. Oakwood was, according to him, a safe town.

Frustrated and feeling overlooked, Rose sighed as she willed her shaking hands to steady. She trudged to the counter to retrieve the doll. It was silly, she knew, but something about it offered solace, peace. She cradled it against her, fighting back the tears and trying to remain sane.

She turned to eye the two men who were still chatting about unimportant things. But when the officer saw her holding the doll, he stopped the conversation, his face icing over. Rose thought she was imagining it until the officer took three steps closer to her, squinting.

"Where did you get that?" he asked, his voice intense for the first time in the whole ordeal. He looked much more concerned than he had been over the blood on the door.

"I-I... it was here when we moved in."

The officer crept even closer, his face near enough that she could see every wrinkle, every scab on it.

"Get rid of it." His words were calm and quiet but menacing all the same. Rose stared at him, confusion and terror rippling through her.

"Get rid of it now," he added before turning back to Thad. The comradery was gone, the good-natured chat. The officer closed his notebook.

"Call me if there are any more incidents," he admitted exclusively to Thad. He turned to eye her warily once more before strolling out the front door.

"I don't understand," she whispered after he was gone.

And for the first time, Thad looked scared, alarmed. "Me neither," he said.

They stood in the kitchen for a long while before eventually, Thad announced he would go out and clean up the mess. She plopped on the couch, rocking the doll and wondering what the hell they were going to do next.

Chapter Eight
Rose
Tuesday Night

She shoved the leftover slices of pizza in the fridge as the music blared. The playlist was supposed to take her mind off of everything, but it was doing nothing of the sort. There was quite a bit of pizza left as she'd not been hungry. She appreciated Thad's frail gesture at bringing normalcy back to the house.

He'd gone back to work after cleaning up the front door. It was even cleaner than it had been before, the shining, white door gleaming in the sunlight. It was like no one had been there. Except someone had, she reminded herself. The shining quality of it was haunting in itself.

It was getting dark out now as the days were getting shorter. She listened to the song about summer blaring on her phone and tried to forget she was here now. She tried to forget a potential psychopath was lurking about.

Thad had insisted he would take Joshua to his basketball game alone. He didn't want to pressure her or trouble her. She knew he didn't want her to be seen, was afraid she'd have what he deemed an episode. Better to offer her up to the wolf at the door with its razor-sharp, bloodied teeth than to parade his wife around town. Image was everything, after all. He would keep her tucked away under the ruse of concern. It would work for outsiders looking in, but it did not fool her. She was just too tired to fight it.

She'd known that about him from the moment they met. He'd disappeared right away to fix his hair and tie on that first official date. He didn't want to look disheveled. She hadn't had the heart to tell him then that perfection wasn't becoming on him. Instead, she'd chocked it up to nerves and told herself it was cute how much he cared. Five years into their marriage, and it wasn't an endearing attribute anymore; it was narcissism cloaked in a nice outfit and a Cheshire cat grin. Still, when life is falling apart, you cling to any sense of normalcy. She wouldn't rock the boat in her marriage now because she didn't have the energy to deal with the shockwaves.

"You heard the officer. Just some teens messing around. Don't let it get to you," he'd ordered her as he kissed her cheek and led Joshua out the door. She was left cleaning up the dinner plates and cold pizza. She was left with their daughter, Lilly, a doll that was apparently a hazard in the town, and a psycho looming at the door. What kind of kid, after all, would smear blood on the door? That wasn't some harmless teenage prank. It was downright disturbing. Why couldn't anyone see that? Maybe she wasn't the crazy one entirely.

She took the pizza box, wondering what to do with it. They hadn't organized their life yet. They didn't yet know where the garbage can would stay outside or where the recycling bin should go. Their lives were a hodgepodge of boxes and mayhem, held together by a man in a business suit and a joint oath to swear off the past. She blinked, inhaled, and headed to the side door to chuck the box onto the deck for now. It would do for this moment. Another day's problem. Thad's problem.

But when she opened the door to the deck, she froze. The pizza box fell out of her hands, and this time, the scream didn't get choked in her throat. It reverberated through the silence of the forest behind her house, a cry in the wind, a prayer in the breeze. Because the sight before her eyes was enough to rattle even the most steadfast person.

There, on the peeling wood of the abandoned deck, was the body of a cat. Orange once, now bloodied, its head was detached. There was no note, no sign, no saying etched in blood. Just a severed cat in pieces on a deck that no one had any business being on.

"What is it, Mama?" Lilly said behind her. She turned around quickly, shutting the patio door and blocking her daughter's sight.

"Nothing, Baby. Go back to the living room. Go get the dolly," she whispered. The doll. The only thing that came to mind. Rose went and claimed it, handing it to her daughter as she swiped away the tears. Lilly didn't take it. She stood, silent and stone-still, as if she could sense the gravity of the situation. Even their five-year-old daughter knew things weren't great. What the hell was wrong with Thad?

Rose was headed to the sofa, still covered in the mover's plastic wrap, with the doll and her daughter when another noise startled her.

The ringtone on her phone blared through the house.

Now what? she thought as she went to claim her phone and deal with whatever was happening now. When she answered the phone and heard the voice on the other end, her heart sank yet again. This was absolutely the last thing on earth a woman in her shoes needed. The very, very last.

Chapter Nine
Rose
Tuesday Evening

"Mother, this really isn't the best time," Rose murmured into the phone swiping a loose strand of hair out of her eyes as she meandered to the kitchen. Her forehead was sweating and her hands shook violently. She wished she had a bottle of wine in the fridge, but Thad hadn't let her bring any. It was a fresh start, after all, he'd reassured her.

"Darling, you sound tired. Are you tired? I knew this move was a terrible idea. Didn't I tell her, Harold?" The voice oozing with condescension resonated in the phone. If she squinted her eyes shut, she knew she could picture her mother in her pearl earrings and perfectly smooth bob standing over their kitchen island as her father, Harold, slouched in the arm chair making faces at her. She was probably tidying the counters or cleaning the fridge as she called, always doing something to ensure the house didn't look lived in. The woman didn't know what rest meant.

It was part of the reason Rose had been more than fine with the move to Oakwood. It put some much-needed distance between her mother and her family. After the incident, her mother had made it her personal mission to tidy Rose's home endlessly, always pointing out the shortcomings. Like she had nothing better to worry about.

"I'm fine. It's just hectic. There's a lot." She regretted the words as soon as she said them, for Susan Elaine Shelby would never let a phrase like that go untouched.

"Why? What is it? Your voice sounds shaky. Are you eating? Sleeping? Do you need me to come down? Just say the word, and I'll have your father drop me off for the week."

"Mother, it's..." She wanted to say "fine." She wanted to tell her mother all was well, but the lie, much like her scream earlier, lodged itself in her throat. Because things weren't fine in so many ways.

"Well, it's just... There were some words painted on our door and now I've found a cat with a severed head. I'm sort of worried, Mother."

"Oh, Dear. I thought it was something really sinister. Harold, it's okay. Just some pranks," she yelled. She hated how her father was always entrapped in the conversation—against his will. It was like having two conversations, one filtered through her mother's willful and judicious lens.

"Well, Mother, the words were painted in blood."

"Are you sure? Because I saw a special on movie magic and did you know Hershey's syrup and food coloring looks just like the real stuff? I bet that's it. Yes, Harold, I'm sure. Hershey's syrup. Yes, it has to be."

Rose closed her eyes, sighing. She wanted to bash her head in. It was pointless to turn to her mother for support. She should've known better than to even try. Suddenly, she envied the poor cat on the deck.

"Yes, I think she's overreacting. Just the anxiety talking and all. Yes, I know," her mother said, not even bothering to wait to gossip about Rose. Only Susan Elaine would have the nerve to do that.

"I'm not overreacting. It turns out the woman who lived here before us, Cloey Fountain, was a bit deranged. I'm trying to piece it together, but apparently something really bad happened here."

"Oh no," her mother said. "Be careful, Rose. You know how you get with this stuff."

"What's that supposed to mean?" she asked, anger surging in her chest.

"Nothing, Dear," her mother replied, muffled for a moment. She was switching the phone to the other shoulder. She was probably getting ready to do dishes while she talked. Rose was never enough to hold her mother's solid attention. "It's just, well, you know how you get obsessed sometimes. Remember when you were convinced that teacher was conspiring against you in junior high? Remember how you snuck out of the house to tail her for a whole evening? Honestly, you've always had this penchant for the dramatic. And with everything that's happened, you just need to be careful. It wouldn't do for you to get caught up in some twisted fantasy. You have a family to think about."

"Mother, I'm fine. I am. I'm just curious is all."

"Well, it's not good that you're alone there all day in that house. Isn't Thad taking some time to help you get settled in? No, no, Harold, he isn't. I know, I know. Always been like that."

"Can you not do that? Talk about Thad like that?" Old resentments bubbled up. Her parents had never accepted Thad. Despite his solid job and stable personality, they'd never liked him. Once a cheater and all that, Susan openly declared whenever given the chance. Her father just thought he was too "pretty" to be the man of the house, his old-school stereotypes worn openly on his sleeve.

Rose wouldn't admit it—ever—but lately, she was a bit resentful that Thad was adjusting so well to Oakwood and leaving her to pick up the pieces. She'd thought a new house would be good for her, but nothing was going as she planned. And now, there was the psycho to worry about. Nonetheless, it was like Thad had moved on already, leaving their old home, their old memories far, far in the past. They were dusty already, coated in a thick, gray muck he didn't dare clean off for fear of getting dirty. They were different like that, she reminded herself. She was more sentimental, he more severed. That was how they worked.

"Well, if you change your mind about this, Darling, you can always come stay with us. It would do you good to be around real family."

"Thad is my family," she argued. Her mother clicked her tongue.

"Well, Rose, I just hope you can find happiness there." The word "there" dripped from her tongue like a poisonous concoction. "After all that you've been through—"

"I love you, Mother. Goodbye," she said, clicking the phone before the woman could get on her soapbox about watchful eyes and lessons learned. She didn't have the time and wasn't in the headspace to hear Susan Elaine's critical observations about parenthood and all the ways Rose had failed.

She knew all of that already. She sank into the couch, exhausted from the call and from her life. She needed to handle the cat. She should probably call the police, but it seemed pointless. Would they even care? They'd probably claim it was a wild animal that had done it. And Thad was too busy to be bothered—he never answered his phone at his son's game. She was alone to deal with it, all alone.

She grabbed the doll, who was abandoned on the couch cushion, and clung to it. Its smooth body rested perfectly in the nook of her arm, and she rocked it, thinking of a time when life was filled with hope and she wasn't so tired. Back and forth, she rocked, perusing the doll's face. Cracked but still beautiful, her face looked up at her, and Rose's heart constricted. She straightened the dress. As she did, she noticed something she hadn't before.

A scratch on the doll's leg peeked out, almost unnoticeable. Feeling a little odd, Rose lifted the fabric more to get a look. There on the doll's thigh, etched recklessly but in tiny, indelible scrawl, was a name.

Evette.

She shook her head, wondering why someone would feel the need to do a tattoo carving on this doll. Is that what Cloey Fountain had named the doll? Had she wanted to brand it as her own? It was all a weird cacophony of questions. Still, as she held the doll to her, she thought maybe there was more to the story. There had to be more. She stood, walking to the deck to go outside and stare at her forest sanctuary when she remembered the cat.

She didn't have the heart or the guts to clean it up. Long ago, she'd lost that audacious, ambitious woman who cleaned up messes without a second thought. She was different now. They all were.

She wondered if wherever Cloey got to, she was different, too. She wondered if she missed the doll, if she used to find solace with it in her arms. She wondered if Cloey Fountain was simply, like so many these days, misunderstood. Sorrow surged in her heart for a woman she didn't know, sorrow the world had not shown to Rose herself.

And, as she walked Lilly back the hall to play, she wondered if there was a way she could find her and tell her thank you for leaving her behind.

Chapter Ten
The Watcher
Tuesday Evening

Her hands shook with a fiery passion. She hated that Rose Taylor had her. She loathed how she clutched it to her chest like it was her *child*. She'd known from the first minute she saw her she was a child snatcher—and worse. The sight of her was just symbolic evidence piled high.

He was never around. She couldn't blame him for disappearing so much. Who wanted to be in the house with a lunatic? A pang of guilt over her word crept into her, a fleeting dragonfly floating on the wind and forgotten about once it took off. She'd been called a lunatic by so many. Maybe it was true. Maybe it wasn't. She didn't care anymore.

She only cared about getting her child back, getting her life back, and exacting justice that the world rarely served. She sank down against the tree, needing to rest her aching legs. The Watcher knew it was her fault. She'd made the choices that led her here. And then she'd made even more choices once she'd gotten to Oakwood. Irrevocable decisions she couldn't take back. Still, she'd come to believe life was for those brave enough to live, to snatch what was theirs, and to run like hell.

That doll, that house, that life—it was not Rose Taylor's to have. Nor should it be any longer. The Watcher was getting impatient. Her body ached with the need to end it. She couldn't be patient much longer.

Still, she'd messed up so many times already in the past six months. She'd almost gotten caught again and again and again. Lurking isn't a job for the feint of heart, she'd learned. She needed to keep the task in focus and keep her head on straight. She would have her child soon enough, and all would be well again.

Once that bitch Rose Taylor was out of the picture.

She wasn't the only bitch, The Watcher knew. There had been so many along the way. There would be others. Sometimes, life felt like an endless pathway of obstacles and speedbumps with fancy manicures. She sometimes felt like doing the good work was impossible. But do it she would.

Being a mother was her highest calling, and that meant making hard decisions sometimes. A mother had to, after all, go to extreme lengths sometimes to protect her child. She would give her child the best. That was what she had always wanted, and that was what no one else could understand.

Her hands shook more noticeably. Maybe it was the loneliness. She was so utterly fucking alone. Her parents had been gone for so long, and he was gone now. It was just her. Her and her child. But right now, her child wasn't in the right place.

She needed to fix that.

The blood and the cat were doing their jobs. Soon enough, he would see the truth; his wife was losing it. Again, panic surged in her chest. She remembered what that felt like all too well. She knew the asylum down the street should be on Rose's mind. She felt a little bad about that. Just a little.

But you did what you had to do. Every woman for herself. That's the way you got through this shitshow thing called life.

She headed back to the van parked in the back to listen to the recording. She'd gotten more advanced this time around, having snuck in to bug the place before the Taylors had made their grand entrance into their new home. It had been easy. Layouts are easy to memorize, after all. She'd put the bugs strategically, hooked up the receiver in her van, and then sat, waiting.

She listened to the conversation Rose had with her mother. She was clearly exasperated with her. Sometimes, the Watcher wondered what would have happened if her own parents hadn't died, if she still had someone to look out for her. Even if they could be annoying, there was a certain comfort in knowing your mother would always have your back.

The conversation didn't give the Watcher any new information other than the fact Rose Taylor was, in fact, cracking. That was good. That was part of the plan. It was easier to kill someone who thought they'd gone mad, she thought. More satisfying. More unexpected. And more deliciously final to kill someone not only in body but also in mind.

She took off the headphones and leaned back in the van's seat. It wasn't as comfy as that first van they'd bought after they got married. He'd insisted they buy what she deemed the Scooby van because of its bluish color. He said it would be perfect for hauling supplies for the remodel they worked on. He also said it would be perfect once they started having kids.

Back when there was hope for their marriage, their life, she thought with a sigh. If only the Scooby van had lived out its full purpose. If only they were still that happy.

But the past was done, and she had new business now. She took a deep breath and demanded herself to focus. Focus, focus, focus. It had always been her strength—and her demise. She got her head on one thing and that was it. That was all she could think about. She could relate to Rose on that part, at least. That part, and loving the feel of motherhood. It was something, she thought.

Maybe in another place, in another time, they could've even been friends. But not here. Not now.

Because now, Rose needed to die. She needed to fucking die before it was too late and the Watcher got caught.

Because then there would be no protecting her child, and the Watcher wouldn't live for that.

Chapter Eleven
Rose
Tuesday Evening

She needed to stay busy, so she decided to chip away at some work. When she unpacked the box in the bedroom, she smiled to see the Monet reproduction she'd always loved. It had been a wedding gift from Thad, one that had made her tear up. He'd paid attention. He'd really paid attention. That was something she wasn't used to with all the men who came before him.

Her fingers traced the rough edges of the frame, dancing over the cheap gold overlay. It was chipping in spots, but she was thrilled at the prospect of having a piece of her old life, the good life, here. Maybe that was it. Maybe she just needed to feel more like this place was home. It never could be completely, but maybe she could try.

She searched box after box for a hammer she knew Thad had to have somewhere, but she kept coming up emptyhanded. Box after box of dishes and décor, of kitchen appliances they'd misplaced and relics of a past version of herself. But no hammer presented itself. Frustration settled in.

She could go to the store and buy a new one, but that would involve getting in the car. That was something she didn't want to think about, even after all this time. She didn't want to take the bus at this hour, her body aching with exhaustion from the day's events. And, in reality, she didn't like the idea of succumbing to the enveloping darkness by stepping foot outside. Someone, after all, could be waiting, watching. At the thought of it, she walked quickly by the bay window in the living room, terrified to glance over and see a menacing face standing watch.

She decided to go to the garage, where Cloey Fountain's belongings had been abandoned. With any luck, perhaps there would be a hammer there and some nails. That seemed like the likely place for it to be. She strolled out the door, reminding herself it was okay, that she would be safe. The garage door was shut. No one could get to her.

Still, the darkness of the garage, even with the lights turned on, made her want to hurry. She walked past abandoned boxes and leftover treasures from a woman she didn't know but longed to. As she entered the back corner of the basement, though, she froze.

Before her, with his distinctive, choppy writing, was the box he'd tried to hide.

Memories.

A simple word for a box full of pain. Still, her heart cracking at the mere thought of what was inside, she ached to open it, itched to see what was inside. It beckoned her to it, the siren's song of masochism. Her fingers caressed the tape.

She didn't need to open the box to know what was on the other side. To open the box would be certain death, danger unprecedented. There was a reason, after all, that Thad had boxed up the items and put them far away. For her safety, he'd noted. For both of their safety.

For her sanity, too, perhaps.

She fought the urge to rip the tape back and to dive into the past. She was stronger than they knew, a fighter deep down. She'd always been the scrappy girl capable of more than anyone could see. She'd fought her way through the loneliness of junior high, through the emptiness of that house she was forced to call home growing up. She overcame heartbreak and setbacks left and right.

This, though. This would be too much. Every fighter has their unwinnable match.

She walked on.

In the back corner, a white, peeling nigh stand caught her eye. It had a few dings on it and a few deep scratches on the top as if someone's fingernails had been dragged across the top. Her hands glanced the surface, feeling the rough wooden texture. Her fingers, slightly shaky from thinking about opening the box, found their way to the metal knob on the front drawer. She pulled it back, not even sure if she was still looking for a hammer. Piqued by nothing but curiosity and an urge to uncover truths, she opened the drawer, slowly, so slowly, the anticipation readily enhancing her heartbeat.

A smattering of objects occupied the drawer. Her fingers pushed past a golden chain with a heart, past a flashlight, and past what looked like a small Bible. Underneath it all, abandoned, was a folded-up piece of paper. The squiggly edges were still on the creased paper, and she felt the urge to rip them off. She pulled out the paper and took it to the center of the garage, squinting to read it but having little luck. She abandoned her search for a hammer, returning to the kitchen to read what was on the paper. A pang of guilt surged in her that she was reading a private note, but she couldn't resist at that point.

She stared at the words etched in an unfamiliar handwriting. Her fingers traced the pen marks, thinking about how they must have been from Cloey Fountain. She imagined red hair pulled back in a ponytail, the doll at her side, as she wrote the words. What was she thinking, and more importantly, what did it mean?

Spread out throughout the paper were details written as though she were in a hurry.

July 8th? 9th?

Janice Waterstone.

Girl.

Room 543.

Night shift. One nurse.

Back entrance.

312.

She glanced over the words over and over as if by osmosis, she could solve the riddle. What did it all mean? July 9th? That was about a month before they bought the place. What happened? What happened to Cloey, or Janice? She needed to sort it out.

To her computer she went, doing a quick Google search.

Janice Waterstone lived in Cedarcrest, which was the town over. And according to the Oakwood Newspaper, there was a birth announcement for July 9th for a little girl. There were no other articles that suggested any ties to Cloey Fountain. There was no mention of a Cloey Fountain, either, she'd doublechecked. It was like the person did not exist, at least in this town.

Maybe this wasn't anything sinister. Perhaps the Fountain girl knew her. But why would she mention the back entrance? The night shift? And why would everyone be so negative about her? Something wasn't sitting right at all.

Room 543 clearly was a hospital room, so Rose searched for the nearest hospital. Cedarcrest and Oakwood shared a hospital right on the Oakwood line called Oakgrove. With Thad and the kids occupied, Rose knew exactly what to do.

IT WAS EASY TO DISMISS someone on the phone, so Rose knew she was doing the right thing to get the answer she needed. She would have to be careful, though. People clammed up at the mere mention of the name. Rose got off the bus and headed inside the unimpressive doors. The hospital was small compared to what she'd seen or expected. She headed inside and asked for directions to the fifth floor—the maternity ward.

For being a small hospital, a palpable buzz of chaos and energy charged the floor as Rose plodded down the shiny tile hallway. The characteristic, antiseptic odor of a medical environment assaulted her nose as she found her way to the front desk.

Medical records were confidential. Every idiot knew that. And it had been a few months since Janice Waterstone had been admitted. It made no sense for her to be there. Still, she would have to hope the small-town vibes would lead to a loosening of protocol and a lack of suspicion.

"Yes?" a nurse drawled, barely looking up from her cup of coffee as she ran a hand through her hair.

"Hi, so sorry to be a bother. I'm here to talk to someone about Janice Waterstone."

At the name, the woman looked up and jumped. After a momentary, blatant panic, she took a breath, her hand resting on her chest as if to assuage her potential heart attack.

"Holy God, you look just like her," she announced. A girl working at a desk behind her turned to look. Her brown eyes were also wide, making Rose feel self-conscious.

"I'm sorry, I'm not sure who you mean. Janice?"

"No. Someone else. Um, I'm sorry, I don't understand what you're looking for Janice for? Are you a reporter?" She bit into the last word like it was a poisonous apple, the crunch echoing in the silence between them.

"Oh, sorry. I'm an old friend of hers and was hoping to see if you happened to have any photos of the baby. I wanted to make a little gift for Janice as a surprise." It was a weak excuse, one she'd concocted on the way. She painted on her most veritable smile, praying it would be enough.

The nurse blinked and shook her head. It clearly was not enough. She stood from her desk, and Rose got nervous.

"First of all," the nurse said, coming out from behind the desk. Rose's heart pounded with terror. "medical records are confidential. Any idiot knows that. Second, I know who you are. The redhead who is new in town, living in Cloey Fountain's old house. You look identical to her. So I don't think you should go poking around making enemies in town. It'll make people nervous. Now get out." She crossed her arms and stood in front of Rose.

"I-I'm sorry," she stuttered, embarrassed for the lie. Certainly, the small-town camaraderie was alive and well in town—but wasn't working in her favor. It had been a fool's errand, like she'd feared.

"Get out before I call security. Don't come snooping around. I don't know what the hell you're up to, Girl, but we'll be watching you. Maybe I'll have to let the police know you were here. Are you in cahoots with that demon girl?"

Rose vehemently shook her head. "No, I'm sorry. I just—I, look. I found this note in a drawer and I wanted to sort it out. I'm sorry for lying." She caved, the mention of the police terrifying her. If Thad found out she was here—she didn't need him thinking all of that again—

The nurse paused, squinting at the note in her hand. Her face stiffened. It did not win her over.

She pointed to the exit. "Get the hell out, and don't you dare come back unless it's because you're in a body bag."

The girl at the desk with braids stood, staring at Rose. Rose nodded, hands in the air, and made a break for the exit. She didn't look turn around.

"ROSE? ROSE TAYLOR, isn't it?" a voice beckoned as she beelined for the bus stop once outside. The air was uncharacteristically chilly for this time of year, and she thought if she puffed enough, she would be able to see her breath. Hands tucked in her pockets, she turned quickly to see who was calling out her name in this strange town.

The girl from the desk, the one with braids, stepped toward her. Rose paused, afraid to move, wondering what now.

"Sorry, I just—a lot of people have mentioned you. Said you moved into her house, right? Into the house on Cedar Street? The one bordering the woods?"

Rose nodded cautiously, glancing back at the bus stop. They were alone, the darkened street quiet.

The girl seemed to sense her wariness. "Look, I just, well, I felt bad for you back there. I thought I could help you. I know what it's like to be new to this town. I didn't grow up here. Moved here five years ago, and I know how the area treats outsiders. Especially in Oakwood."

Rose nodded, seeing a genuine empathy in the girl's doughy eyes.

"I just keep finding so many secrets. I wanted to know what happened is all," Rose said.

The girl nodded, tucking her hands in her pockets now as she got closer. Her voice was barely a whisper.

"People get nervous when you mention her is all. And it doesn't help that you look just like her. It's just, well, she caused a lot of trouble here."

Rose waited for further explanation, wondering what she was about to hear.

"She was here for about six months and didn't really seem like a bother. Troubled, for sure. Carried this weird little porcelain doll around, pushed it in a stroller. She acted like it was a real girl. We all just figured she'd had some trauma, didn't say anything. And things were fine other than that. She got a job at the coffee shop for a while. Was nice enough. Quiet, content even. And then things changed in July."

A car passed by, and both women looked to see who it was before the story continued, as if they were doing something illicit. Maybe, in truth, they were.

"In July, Janice was having her baby here. A little girl. That's when it happened, when Cloey showed her true colors. She broke in the back stairs, got the code somehow. And she took the baby. Right from the hospital. Almost got away with it, too." The nurse looked down at her feet then.

"What happened?"

She sighed, her eyes darting about before landing on her face. "One of our nurses was in the stairwell and saw her. And then..."

An icy pause filled the air.

Rose nodded at her as if willing her on.

She sighed. "The psycho dropped the baby. Just pitched the baby down the steps."

Rose gasped, not expecting that answer for some reason. She shook her head.

"She almost got away, too. Ran past the nurse, shoved her, too. One of our security guards caught her before she could leave town. Said she was raving mad when it happened. Janice said that she'd befriended her at the coffee shop. I guess Cloey was just waiting patiently to snatch the child."

"Holy shit," Rose said, now understanding why everyone was so freaked out by it all. "But when I did some research, I couldn't find anything about the story. No news story."

The girl nodded, shrugging. "Maybe you haven't been here long enough to know this, but Oakwood deals with things a bit differently than most towns. It likes to keep to itself, and, well, some things are just kept secret. No need to panic everyone, the officials figure. They like to keep things quiet, sparkling."

"So what happened to her? Did she go to prison?" Rose asked, finding it all a bit like something out of Black Mirror. No news story? Everything swept under the rug? There had to be more to it all.

"She's gone. That's all we know. I'm not sure if she got away or slipped out of the police's reach or, well, who knows in this place. Oakwood's known for disappearances. Those woods behind you—they're a Bermuda Triangle in their own right.

A chill shot through Rose. It felt like she was hearing some foolish ghost story, some made-up tale meant to scare. Except the girl's eyes looked so serious. She looked at the ground.

"It's why you need to be careful. Don't go asking questions. Don't go searching for answers to questions you don't want to know. People in this town don't look kindly on people, especially outsiders, who insert their nose in others' business. The town likes to keep things quiet, smooth. Don't get in the way of that."

"Or what?" Rose asked, wrapping her jacket around her more tightly.

The girl said nothing, just shaking her head. "You need to be careful. Everyone's watching you already. The red hair doesn't help. Keep to yourself. Stop questioning it all. Like I said, those woods are dangerous. People sometimes go into them and don't come back."

Rose opened her mouth to ask something else, but the girl spun on her heel and left. She didn't look back. Rose forced her feet to plod to the bus stop, keeping her coat wrapped tightly around herself the entire time. Every town, every person, every family had secrets. She knew this all too well. But somehow, Oakwood's secrets seemed poisonous.

And she was no longer certain if Cloey Fountain was the aggressor—or the victim.

Chapter Twelve
Rose
Tuesday Night

Propped against the headboard with their bedroom lamp resting on an unpacked box, Rose picked at a piece of her fingernail as Thad got into bed. He had been late with the kids, and with nighttime routines, she hadn't had a chance to tell him her discoveries. Anxiety riddled her as she thought about what she knew and how to tell him.

He leaned in to perfunctorily kiss her cheek. His lips lingered slightly, as if he wanted more but knew better than to ask these days. Intimacy had slipped from their marriage when that horrid day happened. She sighed as she turned to him.

"What's wrong?" he asked.

Everything. Absolutely everything. But as with so many other times, she choked back her true words and, instead, looked at him. He reclined against the pillows. She sat up straighter.

"I found out some disturbing news today about Cloey Fountain," she said matter-of-factly.

He shook his head and stared at her. "Who?"

"Cloey Fountain. The woman who lived here before us."

"Oh, okay," he answered. He sat straight up now, also propped against the headboard. They sat like a couple in the same booth at a restaurant but without the connection and understanding that seating arrangement typically denoted.

She told him the story. She left out how she'd come to get the information, not wanting to hear his accusations.

"That sounds like a tall tale. I mean, if that were true, it would be in the newspaper, or we would've heard about it. I don't think the town is going to cover it up collectively," he said dismissively. Just like he always did.

"Thad, I'm serious. It's true. And I do think there's more to this town that we've seen. It's all a bit sketchy. The way she just disappeared into the night."

"How did you come across this information?" he asked. A tinge of accusation burned in his words. She uncovered herself and stood in her nightgown, crossing her arms across her chest as she suddenly felt too bare. She sauntered to the window, leaning against the chilled glass as she looked out into the moonlit forest.

"I found a note that led me to the hospital. And then, I did some questioning. But it's true, Thad. She tried to kidnap a baby and ended up killing her. Dropped her down the stairs. The security guards caught her. But then she disappeared. There's no mention of it in the newspaper, no trial. No front page news. She just vanished. And no one will say where she is. Isn't it all just bizarre? And the way the town talks about her, the threatening tone. It freaks me out." She turned to look at her husband who hadn't made a single move to approach her.

His eyes perused her, judgingly, scathingly even. She squirmed under his condescending look.

She walked forward, two steps, then three. She stood over the bed, looking down at him.

"It's all true. I know you think I'm crazy. But it's true. And that means we're not safe here, Thad. We're not safe after all."

Now it was his turn to sigh. "I don't think you're crazy, Rose. It's just—you've been through a lot. We've been through a lot. And I don't want you to go down a dark path again."

"What path would that be? The truth?" she asked.

Now, he did get up and stood on the other side of the bed. The gulley between them felt deathly wide and scandalously sharp.

"The path that leads you to becoming obsessed. You know you do that, Rose. You get an idea in your head, and it consumes you. It's part of the reason we left Trentsville."

She shook her head, disbelieving of his nerve.

"You said we left for a fresh start."

"We did. And you and I both know you couldn't have it there. You couldn't put it behind you. You couldn't put her behind you if we were there. And you couldn't put my past to bed, either. You were always looking over your shoulder, always trying to figure it out."

Tears started to stream now at the mention of it all as anger surged.

"And what do you do that's so much better, Thad? Huh? Pour yourself into your work? Toil away at the office until your past is just a distant memory and nothing bothers you? Pretend she isn't a danger to us all, protect her by ignoring it? Pretend we haven't lost it all?"

"It's not the same."

"No, it's not. Because when you become obsessed, you attribute it to being driven. When I get obsessed with something, you determine its madness. Double standards. Just like she always said. You have a double standard, ridiculous standards for everyone around you."

His fist slammed on the box, rattling the lamp until it fell over.

"Fuck you, Rose. Fuck you."

He stormed out of the room, slamming the door so hard, it rattled. She was certain it would wake Lilly, but the little girl didn't come running. She didn't make a sound. And Joshua was used to this sort of arguing. It scared her to think it had become part of the norm.

She returned to the window and looked out into the forest, wondering if this was how Cloey felt.

Alone in the darkness, the vast wilderness stretched before her as a harbinger she couldn't avoid.

A crow cawed in the distance as she leaned her head against the glass and said a prayer she hadn't said in a while.

Chapter Thirteen
The Watcher
Wednesday Morning

The crow's caw made her jump. She scolded herself for being so jumpy. Staring up at the house, she could see her, standing like an abandoned widow looking forlornly into the forgotten moonlight. She'd heard the door slam from even here. He wasn't happy. They were breaking. That was exactly what she needed.

A weak relationship meant it was easier to strike. She'd learned that firsthand. This time, though, it would work to her advantage.

It served Rose right. Certainly, the Watcher had made her share of mistakes, at least in the eyes of others. There was no denying that. Some might even call her dangerous, deadly. But everything she did, she did for that elusive yet poignant title: mother. It always came back to that, something so many would never understand. Something Rose could never comprehend because, quite frankly, she was clearly a terrible one.

The crow cawed again, another joining in and creating a sinister cacophony, a funeral dirge that rattled even the most steadfast soul. The eeriness of the noise, though, energized her. She inhaled deeply, the scent of dirt and mildew reminding her of a time that was long ago yet somehow felt right in front of her.

The way his hand wrapped around hers. The stamp of forever marked in his eyes. The wooded path ahead of them, the moonlight shimmering golden as the crows cawed back then, announcing the arrival of the gilded couple. The feeling of forever wrapped up in his hand, the businessman who had claimed her as his own, despite her humble roots. They were in love then—weren't they? What happened? Even after all of these months of pondering, years in truth, she had no idea.

That was, perhaps, the most enraging of all.

She dropped back, not wanting to push her luck. She was too close to the grand finale now. The knife buzzed in her jeans' pocket. The severed head tied around her belt clinked against her, the foul smell swirling about and bringing her back to the present. Things were different now.

A scream echoed through the forest, this one not from a bird. She'd heard talk of how these woods were haunted, the local lore depicting tales of long claws and frightening freaks who wandered about. Ambling toward the van, though, the relic of terror still clinking against her leg, she exhaled the truth in her heart.

She knew, after all, the real haunting was what happened in your heart, your head, and in the space between you and one you could no longer have.

Chapter Fourteen
Rose
Wednesday Morning

Footsteps. Running footsteps on the deck.

Rose bolted upright in bed, tossing the covers off as she reached for her phone instinctually. She'd been dead asleep, having gone back to bed after she'd seen Lilly and Thad off to work. She'd been tired, perhaps coming down with whatever flu or illness that had kept Joshua home from school that morning.

She tried to convince herself she'd been dreaming. But no. She was certain. *Tromp, tromp, tromp.* The footsteps had been distinctive and clear, echoing on the deck boards that wrapped around the back of the house close to her bedroom window. She flung back the covers and dashed to the hallway, breathing heavily.

Her fingers poised over the number 9, ready to dial. But she thought about the town's icy reception to her, how she had been already gaining a reputation for asking so many questions. It wouldn't do for them to think the new woman in town was crazy. They'd been dismissive of the blood on the door, writing it off as nothing but kids. And until they got to the house, whoever it was would be gone.

Her heart pounded. She knew what she had to do.

Maybe it was just Cloey Fountain coming back for her stuff. Somehow, that made her feel better, like there was an ally out there—which was insane because Cloey Fountain, if rumors were to be true, was no one's ally.

Another subtle thought crept into her head, one she wanted to silence. It had been rippling in the back of her mind. But it couldn't be that. No way. There were too many miles between them now.

She tiptoed through the house, her feet still not quite certain of the steps in the new territory. She made her path to the patio door though. Mercifully, it was closed. But her eyes landed on a streak of red running down the glass. Splatters of red were sprinkled all over the once shiny glass, but no words spelled out any dire messages. She peeked through the glass, tiptoeing up.

She opened the sliding glass door carefully, the phone still poised in her hand.

No one was there. She looked left and right, then left again. And then it happened.

A figure dressed in black crept out from under the deck. Rose emitted a scream, but it all happened too fast. Something flew at her head at what felt like the speed of sound. The figure, wearing a Halloween mask, dashed through the woods, nimble and surefooted. Rose touched the gooey substance on her cheek as she stared at the deck, the severed head of a squirrel rolling at her feet. Tears filled her eyes. What did they want? What did they want with her?

She sank to her knees, hysterical now and terrified. Death was all around her, it seemed. She couldn't even talk let alone dial the phone.

"What is it?" a deep voice beckoned from the door. Joshua. He extended a hand, uncharacteristically helpful.

Her sobs racked her body.

"Come on, let's go inside," he murmured.

"N-no. There's someone out there. I saw them."

Joshua didn't reply, though. Instead, he shoved her toward the door. "Let's get inside. It will be fine."

"I'm telling you the truth."

"Okay, Rose. Okay."

She shook her head, but he was a strong boy.

"Let's get inside and lock the doors. It'll be fine." He talked to her as if she were a child to be placated, but she was too tired to fight. Her hands were shaking as she sat at the kitchen table.

"We need to call the police," she whispered. "We do." She needed to protect what was left of her family.

"It's fine, Rose. It's fine. I'll make you some tea." His actions were kind, but they were masked by a coldness in his voice. He'd never let her in. Five years still wasn't enough to let her in. Sadness clouded her thoughts over this. She would never be his mother.

She tried to calm herself, to tell herself maybe he was right. Perhaps she'd imagined it all. Joshua made her a cup of tea in the microwave, and she warmed her hands. She thought about calling Thad, but he had an important meeting today. She couldn't keep bothering him at work if she wanted him to keep his job. It was broad daylight. She would be okay, wouldn't she? It was probably still those damned teenagers, she told herself.

Still, she got up after a while and walked to the bedroom. She rooted in an unpacked box and found it. Her baseball bat. She'd always been afraid of guns since she was a little girl, but the bat made her feel safe. Thad thought it was ridiculous. She wouldn't be able to overpower an ant, he'd always teased. But clutching the weapon and looking out the window, she felt like she could channel enough rage into the bat to be effective.

She breathed in and out, like her old therapist suggested. In and out. Count to five. Stay grounded in reality.

As she closed her eyes and focused on her senses, she heard murmuring. Joshua's voice rang out through the semi-empty house. She walked closer to his room, listening.

"I know. I'm fine. Yes, I'll talk to Dad about it. I miss you, too, Mom. Soon. Hopefully soon."

Shit. Of course the bastard had turned on her. He'd called his mother to report on her insanity. That horrible woman would use this, certainly she would use this. In court for a custody hearing. She would try to get Joshua back because of this and then Thad really would lose it on her.

She dashed into the room and grabbed the phone from her stepson. She clicked the end call button. "What are you doing?" she asked, staring at him as she tossed his phone on his bed.

He took a step forward. "What the hell are *you* doing? I'm allowed to talk to her, you psycho. You don't own me."

Rose felt her heartbeat run wild again, thinking about Jade, Thad's first wife. She thought about all of the shady shit that had happened, about how much safer she felt with distance between them.

"Well, I don't like you talking to her. For obvious reasons."

"Yeah. Because you're a lunatic," he murmured. She felt her fingers tense and ball into a fist. She held herself back. She breathed in and counted again. She needed to be patient with him. That was how she would win him over.

"I'm sorry about earlier. You're right. It was probably nothing," she announced. She didn't need Joshua telling Thad, too. She didn't need the three of them, the family of the past, ganging up on her. She would handle it herself.

"I'm going back to sleep," he murmured without even looking at her. She suspected he would call her again once she was out of the room. There wasn't much she could do about that. She returned to the living room. Evette was perched in her stroller by the television, staring at her with those soulful eyes as if asking where she'd been. Rose needed comfort, and the doll did that for her. She picked her up.

"There, there. We'll figure it all out," she murmured, wiping at her hair.

She held the doll for a long time, trying to avoid looking out into the forest. She left the smears of blood on her cheek, not caring in the least who saw it.

Chapter Fifteen
Rose
Wednesday Morning

Joshua kept sleeping, and Rose was secretly glad to not have to face him. Theirs had always been a complex relationship that just kept intensifying as he got older, as his mother fed him more lies, and as the distance between them continued to spread.

Still, she found herself enveloped in terror as she stood in the house in silence. She wanted to watch the woods, to see if she could see anything, yet she couldn't get up the nerve. A part of her wanted to go back to bed, put her head under the covers, and pretend life was perfect. But she'd played that game for many months, and it had left her stranded and empty.

Thus, she decided to busy herself. Nothing she could do about the severed head or the watcher of the woods now. She would stay tucked away inside, the comforts of home around her—or at least the ones she'd bothered to unpack. She could understand how so many developed a phobia of going out. Outside was dark and filled with squirrel mutilators.

She decided to tackle the boxes in the living room, the ones in the corner away from the door. Every once in a while, as she worked, she would imagine someone standing up against the glass, pressed up to it like a villain from a bad horror movie. Rose would, in those moments, glance over her shoulder and take inventory. But it was always empty. Dark and empty. She returned to her work.

Sweat soaked her shirt as she labored away, rooting through boxes and unpacking items from a life no longer hers. How many vases, knickknacks, pottery pieces would it take to make it feel right? Like a home? The clutter suffocated her, and she realized she didn't want to create a museum to commemorate the past Rose Taylor. She closed up the box she was working on and made the decision to stow it away.

She lugged the box up the stairs, finding the pull-down stairs she'd seen on her first tour of the house. The stairs creaked down, and she thought perhaps she'd wake Joshua. He did not stir, though, or perhaps continued to selectively ignore the happenings of the house in favor of whatever was keeping him company. The steps stood before her like a wooden mecca, a temple she didn't know if she could climb. She tossed the box onto the third stair as she precariously climbed the dusty wooden steps. Darkness poured out from above, but she pushed herself onward. There was nothing scarier than the past now.

Once in the attic, she tossed the box down. Some light streamed in through the dirty windows of the attic. It was cut into by the tapering of the roof so that it was impossible to stand fully except in the very mid-point. She stayed seated on the splintery floor, letting her feet dangle as she looked around, half expecting to see a dead animal or some sort of satanic setup. Perhaps a bag of bones.

Instead, though, she saw a box. Discreet and utilitarian, the box sat perfectly crisp and folded, as if it had been recently placed in the confines of the attic. It seemed as though it weren't even up there long enough to absorb the musty, archaic odor an attic offers its relics. Curiosity got the better of her. She crawled forward, relenting herself to the possibility of splinters and dust in favor of seeking the truth.

Her fingers carefully peeled open the box. Her eyes perused the contents, which were upsettingly unremarkable.

An album. A single album resting in the cardboard sanctuary. She did not stop to ponder as she plucked it eagerly from its tomb, her fingers flipping through.

The images were startling. Disturbing. Cryptic.

Photograph after photograph of Evette in all sorts of poses. Different outfits. Several on the sofa, one by what looked like a bottle. Some in the yard, sprawled out on a baby blanket in the summer sun. A few photos of the doll in a stroller by the edge of the forest, as if abandoned for her own good. Photograph after photograph lined the album. Some had captions that simply consisted of a date. The still form of the baby, although lifelike, certainly seemed out of place because Rose knew the truth. It was a doll. Who would go to this much trouble to photograph a doll, and why? It didn't sit well within. It creeped her out, in truth.

But as she flipped through the pages, a stark reality started to settle over her and cloak her goodwill. It wasn't upsetting because it was weird, she realized. It didn't bother her that this album, whoever it belonged to, was left in the attic as if it awaited her. It wasn't even the eerie photo of the doll in a bathtub that sent her over the edge. It was something else.

Jealousy.

For as she stared at the photos, she realized she was bothered by the fact that someone else had laid claim to Evette, someone else had held the doll and cradled it as her own. It hurt to think of a time when it wasn't hers. It made Rose want to cling to the sweet angel tighter, to never let her go.

Why had she let go?

She closed the album, considered burning it, and then tossed it to the bowels of the attic to be hopefully forgotten. These photographs wouldn't see the light of day. They'd be left right where they belonged—forgotten in the dust so that new memories could be made.

Rose had her chance to try again, she realized. It would be different, but it was a chance all the same.

Chapter Sixteen
Rose
Wednesday

"It's been six months. You can't keep this up. We can't keep this up," he said, his voice deceptively calm. Still, as she rocked Evette in her arms, she could sense the accusatory tone to his voice.

He'd come home at lunch with a smile on his face. She'd been standing in the living room, looking out the patio doors as she rocked the doll. It felt so good to have her in her arms. Her Evette. Hers.

She'd turned to see him, the fitted suit on his body and the confident smile on his face. He'd beelined for her and kissed her cheek. He'd loosened his tie and tried to grab the doll from her. It had been clear what was on his mind—but she was surprised. The middle of the day? After everything? Her body tensed. It'd been so long.

She'd clutched the doll tighter to herself. "Joshua is home," she said in a hushed whisper.

"And we have our own room with a locking door. He's sleeping, isn't he? We'll be quiet. And quick." He again reached for the doll. She'd stepped back, out of his reach, where she humbly aboded for months now. She'd stared up at him as his face fell.

Now, she felt her chest heave as he said the words. Six months. Six fucking months. Had it only been that long? Some days, it felt like a lifetime. Sometimes, it felt like it was yesterday that she'd collapsed with it all.

Regardless, sex was the last thing on her mind. The very, very last.

"I'm sorry," she said now, half meaning it. "I just can't. There's too much."

He sighed audibly and stepped back, turning his back to her. She turned to look out the window. But she gasped when, in a few quick, angry strides, he was right next to her cheek again.

"You have to move on. It isn't fair to either of us. I know it's hard, but it's hard for me too, dammit. I'm trying here. Are you?"

She could not bring herself to turn and look into those eyes for she was afraid she would see what she didn't want to see.

The eyes of a desperate man, a man ready to give up.

She stared into the forest as he breathed heavily beside her. The words of her father echoed between her ear and the glass.

"Once a cheater, always a cheater. That man's a scoundrel. What are you thinking?"

She'd been pissed at him then. Had sworn to choose Thad over everything. Now, though, she thought with a harsh slap in the face from reality, that her father was right.

Scoundrel.

Cheater.

Cheater again?

She rocked the doll as he stomped away. It wasn't fair. He'd been through hell and back, too. And just because he got back up quicker, just because he was standing again—it wasn't fair to hold that against him, was it?

She wanted to fall into his arms like old times, to promise to love him better. She wanted to beg him to be patient for a while longer, to swear to him she'd get better. But holding the doll as she stared into the forest, she worried that the space between them was too great. The strain was too much. And, at the heart of the matter was this—it was her fault. She'd been the one to fail him, them, the family.

"I'm sorry," she murmured, but when she turned to look, he was already heading out the door. He would leave her. She knew it. He would leave her just like he left Jade. He would find someone new, someone exciting, someone better. She'd be left in the ashes of them, picking up the scattered pieces she didn't even think belonged together anymore.

She pulled Evette to her breast and leaned her back against the glass, reveling in how fragile and cold it felt. She closed her eyes, the doll in her arms, and thought of a different time. A stronger time. A time when all was right in the world.

Chapter Seventeen

Rose

Wednesday Afternoon

"Can you take me to school?" Joshua asked her, emerging from his room after Thad left. "I'm feeling fine now."

She eyed him suspiciously, wondering if he'd heard any bits of their argument. His eyes were dead, though, and he didn't make eye contact with her. That was nothing new.

"Yes. I'll walk you to the bus stop," she said, balancing Evette on her hip.

"Can't we just drive?" he asked.

She gave him a Medusa level look. He shook his head and mumbled under his breath, returning to his room to get ready. She tucked Evette into the stroller and grabbed her bag.

When Joshua came out of the room, he looked at her with disdain. "I'll just walk myself," he offered.

She shook her head. "No. Not with everything happening lately. I'm going with you," she assured him. They weren't close by any means. But she loved him, and Thad loved him. She wouldn't let anything happen. She couldn't let it be like last time.

"Can you leave that at home then?" he asked, gesturing toward the stroller and the doll.

She shook her head. "It's fine."

"It's not fine. I don't want to be the laughing stock of the neighborhood again." He stood with his hands in his pockets. Something about the way he looked at her reminded her of Thad. She was tired of being talked down to, the family crazy.

"I'll take whatever I want with me. Now let's go." She moved toward the door with the stroller. Joshua slammed his hand against the wall and then, like a raging wolf, scampered toward the stroller. He grabbed the doll from the seat and tossed it into the middle of the living room.

"I said fucking leave it," he bellowed, rage shaking his voice. He sounded like a man trapped in a boy's body.

She stood stoic for a second, her heart beating from the unexpected. But then, she stepped forward, grabbing his arm. "Don't tell me what to do."

"I'm calling my mother. I'm telling her to come get me. You're batshit crazy. You're the batshit one," he yelled, tears now streaming down his face.

And it all crashed down. The doll, the threats. The word batshit itself.

Batshit crazy.

That's what they'd all said.

That was Jade, not her. Couldn't they see?

She would never hurt someone, she told herself through the racking sobs. Never. She hadn't meant to hurt her then. She hadn't meant to be a bad mother, and she didn't mean it now. But she couldn't stop herself. The stress of the past six months, the condescension in their eyes. She was losing everyone. Everyone, everyone, everyone.

It all whirled into a cataclysmic event that ended with one fatal, instinctive, reactive choice.

A slap.

She slapped Joshua's face, the crack a satisfying but indelible mark in the air between them. He yowled, and then spun on his heal. She reached out toward him but then put her hand back in its normal space. It was done. She'd done it. She couldn't take it back.

She wanted to sink to the floor, the cry into a puddle of who she was becoming. But she couldn't. Evette needed her. She crossed the room to the abandoned doll and scooped her up.

"There, there," she whispered. "I'll protect you."

As she rocked the baby and sang a song about moonlight to her, she heard Joshua's voice, muffled in the other room. He was calling for help. She no longer cared.

She no longer cared about hardly anything.

Chapter Eighteen

Rose

Wednesday Afternoon

"What's wrong with you?" he screamed, holding her against the glass of the patio door. His forearm stabbed into her chest, pushing on her neck until she wondered if this was where it would end. He would break her neck. She deserved it.

Tears dropped.

"He was being so mean. He was being so rude to me," she said.

"That's not a fucking excuse, Rose. It's gone too far now. You've gone too far. I know you're grieving, but hitting my son is too much." He attacked the words like a hunter chasing prey, biting into each syllable meticulously. But all she heard was the phrase that told the entire saga: "my son." Not theirs. Not hers. "My son." There would always be that distinction living between them. Jade would always have that claim. She would not.

Her father had always brough that up. How she would never own his whole heart because of his past. "Once a man gives his heart to someone and has a child, there is no claiming him. No matter what." These had been the words he'd uttered before their wedding night, when he'd begrudgingly gave her away to a man he didn't believe in.

Back then, she'd been lost in the wistful quality of their romance. She'd believed Jade was the villain and that Thad deserved more—he deserved her. She would do anything to make him happy, even if it meant taking on a stepson she barely knew. A stepson who held the wreckage of his family against her.

Now, she knew how wrong she was.

"It's been hard, Thad. I'm struggling," she said. It came out like an excuse, though, instead of the cry for help she'd meant it to be.

"We're all struggling, here. You're not the only one who lost that night, you know that, right? Or have you forgotten?"

"You seem fine to me," she said as he loosened his grip. He shook his head wildly.

"Because I have no choice. Someone has to keep it fucking together."

"I suppose that's my fault, too," she whispered.

He stepped back, throwing his hands in the air as he clenched his jaw. "Unbelievable. Always the victim. Always. Can't you see what you're doing to us? This didn't have to wreck us. It didn't. It's hard, and it's awful. But we could've done it together."

She noted the past tense. Past tense was never a good thing when it came to love.

"But now, you're fucking hitting my son. You realize she could get custody back, don't you? And then where will be?"

"Does it matter? Does any of it matter?" Tears flowed copiously now. She couldn't breathe, couldn't think. She stared at the man who was more stranger than partner now, who perhaps always was.

He ran a hand through his hair. "I'm going to lose my job if this keeps up. Do you realize that? I'm going to lose it."

"Well, it's not my fault you came home twice now." She angered at the thought of him coming home to claim her at lunch, thinking she owed him that.

"It is your fault. Don't you see? I can't trust you being at home alone. And every day, you have the cops here with some outlandish story or you're hitting my son. He's scared, you know. He thinks you're off his rocker."

Like his mother. The words hang-glided in the air between them, and she sputtered on them.

"It's not my fault you didn't love her as much as me, apparently," she spewed. And then his hands were around her neck again, her back against the glass. Her throat ached so much, she thought the bones in her neck cracked. Her throat was closing, and the air wouldn't leak in. She stared into his sweating, growling face and wondered how it had come to this.

The corners blackened.

"You're a terrible mother," he bellowed, spit flying from his mouth as he screamed at the top of his lungs. And then, silence. She couldn't cry, couldn't argue. Couldn't even whimper. Her hand tapped pathetically against the window, but he wasn't watching for any signs to stop. Maybe she didn't want him to.

Because the truth rang out like a sad gong being whacked over and over.

Terrible. Mother.

Terrible. Mother.

His hands loosened slightly. Gasp. Choke. Pain.

How could she?

How could she not watch?

How did she let it happen?

I'm sorry.

The blackness opened up. Breathe.

Gasp.

Breathe.

It's not okay.

It all hurt. Her throat hurt. She needed more air.

Bad Mother. Terrible Mother. Undeserving.

He let go, and she crumbled to the ground, choking and sputtering. She clasped her throat as if to make sure it was still there. Everything was spinning and wild. She stared at his too-shiny shoes.

He said nothing and she couldn't, numbed to the present but burning in the ashes of the past.

The crushing truth sliced her open. She was a terrible mother. She'd been one then; she was one now. He would leave her. He would cheat on her and leave her and she'd be all alone. There would be no one to save her, not even herself.

"I'm sorry," she weakly whispered after a long moment. But she doubted he could see through his anger that she meant it. She truly meant it all.

He slammed his hand down on the counter. And then, he did what he did best.

"He'll leave you," her father's distant words echoed in her mind.

Sure enough, Thad did.

Chapter Nineteen

Rose

Wednesday Afternoon

She'd put on a high-neck sweater even though the day didn't warrant it. She was too afraid of people seeing the redness, the marks. Even after all that had transpired, she protected him. They all did, didn't they? That was the curse of loving the charming, the go-getter—no one could see the darkness looming within. The wooden bench seemed to cradle her as the soft sunshine streamed through. Evette sat in her stroller, looking up at her with knowing eyes. Rose reached out and touched the baby's hand, comforted by how peaceful she looked. At least someone looked serene.

A few dog walkers passed by on the sidewalk at the little park. She'd walked, of course, not really aiming for anywhere in particular except anywhere but the house. She could not be there in that prison cell of condescension, doubt, and danger. After Thad had left, Joshua in tow, Rose had picked up baby Evette and headed out the door. She'd surveyed the front and side yard for the person who was messing with her. At this point, though, her own house was in such disarray that it hardly seemed like the biggest threat was from the outside. It was from the inside looking out.

She'd walked about the quiet town of Oakwood, staring at white picket fences and manicured lawns and mailboxes that screamed "traditional." She knew all too well, though, that every front door potentially hid acidic truths—tales of deceit, betrayal, vengeance, and dismay. This thought did not comfort her—sometimes misery doesn't actually want company, in truth. Sometimes it just wants to escape.

When she'd come across this small park, she'd sat at the bench by the swing set. Lilly loved the swings. She longed now to hear her chorus of "higher, higher, higher," but was also glad Lilly hadn't witnessed the physical undoing of them. There was a blessing in that.

A woman approached Rose, interrupting her morbid thoughts.

"Seat taken?" she asked, studying Rose. Rose didn't bother to look up at her. She didn't want company but nodded to be gracious.

A moment of quiet contemplation passed between the two strangers. Finally, the woman spoke up. "Nice day, huh?" she asked.

Rose fought the urge to roll her eyes. Her life was imploding, and this annoying woman wanted to discuss the weather. She wasn't buying it.

She said nothing, gently pushing the stroller with her free hand.

"My little Mary loves coming here to swing, no matter what the weather is. Last week, we were here in the rain. Do you come here often?" Her tinny voice grated on Rose's nerves. She turned to look at the woman, finally, assessing her zipped up hunter green jacket, her hair in a low bun, and her too bright lipstick.

"You must know who I am. Everyone in town seems to know I'm new."

The woman's lips parted, and it was clear the wheels were turning. Finally, she coughed, and said, "Sorry. I didn't want to seem creepy. But yes, you're right. Oakwood keeps tabs on newcomers. We knew you were coming probably before you did," she said, laughing.

Rose offered her a weak smile. It was the best she could do.

"Anyway, yes, I've heard about your family moving into 312 Cedar. The house, as I'm sure you know, has somewhat of a reputation." At this, she glanced down at Evette, at the stroller. She tensed up slightly, her hands gripping the bench. Rose delighted a bit in the fact she could stir that reaction in the woman.

"So do you have kids?" she asked, eyeing Rose.

Rose was still pushing the stroller. "Yes. A daughter, Lilly. She's at school right now. I promised her I'd take care of her new doll." It wouldn't do to spill everything to this woman, to tell her the doll was more of a comfort object than anything these days. It wouldn't do to tell her that her husband had almost choked the life out of her, that someone odd was messing with her, that her husband's ex-wife was a stalkerish disaster, that her step-son hated her, that she'd hit him, and that six months ago—

It wouldn't do at all.

The woman, who had yet to divulge her name, seemed satisfied with the explanation. Rose could tell by the woman's sigh of relief she'd been worried, as if the doll were cursed or something. Madness didn't haunt dolls—it ran through marriages, motherhood, and womanhood, though. Still, if the perfect clones in Oakwood could believe that madness was something held in a relic, an object, a cursed belonging, they would believe the lie that they were at a safe distance from it.

"Is the move going okay?" The mother turned her attention to the blonde girl for a moment after the words were out.

"Look how high!" the little voice chirped, and Rose felt her heart lodge in her throat. She looked away.

"As good as it can be. Sort of a mess, of course, with Cloey leaving in a hurry."

Rose could practically feel the woman's heart stop at the mention of the name. Maybe she should've hid her hand longer, but she was sick of tiptoeing.

"Yes, not a great situation there. But we're glad you're here now instead of her. That was a real mess."

"Uh huh. Except it's so odd that she just sort of disappeared, don't you think?" She turned now to watch the woman squirm at the mention. She clearly looked paler, her eyes darting about.

"Well, you know how crazy is." And then she paused, realizing the err in her words. "I didn't mean—"

"No, no. Of course not. But the thing is, even crazy has to go somewhere. It doesn't just vanish, does it?"

A moment of pause, a moment of assumed debate on the woman's part.

"I don't know. But, well, Oakwood seems to be a disappearing point sometimes, you know? Those woods behind your house—not to scare you—but people disappear there sometimes. Who knows?"

Rose's attention was sparked. She thought of the beheaded animals, the eerie message. A cruel reality settled into her bones. Oakwood wasn't safe. They'd blamed Cloey Fountain for that, but she was gone. So who was the true culprit?

"Really?"

"Yes. Look, I know we don't know each other well, but hear me out on this. Don't go in those woods." She bit her lip, as if fighting the deluge of words. They were uncontrollable now, though.

"Why not?" she prodded when the woman stopped.

She sighed, her eyes appraising the area. There was no one except the two of them, a doll, and the child on the swing.

"People talk. Legends. Creepy legends. One talks of a creature living there, which is outlandish, of course. But well, I do think there's something sinister at play there. For a while, there was a rumor of a serial killer living out there in that forest. Others, still, think that some of the lunatics from the asylum get out."

"Asylum?" This was news.

"You haven't heard? Redwood Asylum. Well, Redwood Psychiatric Hospital to be accurate, but we all know what it is. It's been there forever. Sort of a guarded secret, though. The town doesn't like to talk about it."

"Why not?" she asked, curiosity heightened. She readjusted on the bench, her hand leaving the stroller.

The woman shrugged. "People talk. There have been a few escapees over the years. And, well, let's just say it's not a place you want to go. It houses really tough cases. Criminally insane. People who have done horrible things."

"And it's near my house?" A chill reverberated through Rose.

"Yes. Not far actually. Through the woods a ways. I used to live on your street, but the sightings and the stories got to be too much. There were cases of people disappearing out there, which only fuels the rumors. I just didn't like the idea that if someone escaped from the asylum, they'd be right there, watching. It gave me the creeps."

Rose shivered at the thought. It couldn't be, could it? She thought of the prickling sensations, the watching feelings. The beheadings and blood. The dismissive attitude of the police.

Her mind got to racing.

"Can you visit this place?"

"I don't know why you'd want to. But no, they don't really take visitors except family for some of the lesser cases. It's a private place. You don't want to go snooping. There's a reason you didn't know it was here. No one really does. Besides, I was there once to pick up a friend who works there. The screams—they stick with you in your nightmares."

"The screams?"

"Yes. The screams of the living—but also the dead. They say it's haunted. Another reason to steer clear."

Rose felt like she was on the set of some ridiculous movie, suddenly. A haunted asylum? People disappearing? What the hell kind of place were they in? What kind of alternate reality did Thad move them to?

Danger lurking inside. Danger lurking out. Rose began to realize what she'd learned so many times in life—safety was relative, and really, it was nowhere.

"Thanks," she told the stranger and got up and left. She realized she had yet to catch her name, but it no longer mattered.

Chapter Twenty
The Watcher

T*en.*
   He didn't love her anymore. Hadn't loved her for a while. The words asphyxiated her. A heavy vat of poison drowned her as he said the words so, so calmly across the table. When had it happened? Sure, things had been rocky. But when did she go from being his world to being the woman he couldn't trust, couldn't possibly love? When did her shortcomings become turnoffs and her strengths become his weaknesses?

She felt her whole life melt into that toxic wasteland as he murmured on about friendships and broken, about failed forevers and better paths. She knew, though, even when her heart was cemented to the ground by his words, she would never love anyone as much as him. She never could. She would spend her days pining for him. The only question was—how to make him pay for it?

And then he was gone, and she was the one holding the weapon. She was the one left cleaning up the bloody mess.

Nine.

Motherhood. It was all she ever wanted. From the time she held that doll in her arms as a child, she wanted to hold the real thing, call the real thing hers. She burned to be a mother. She thought of nothing else. He had done that for her—and then he'd ripped the title from her. Sure, he would say it wasn't his fault. He would blame her erratic behavior, if he was asked about it. He would claim she deserved it all. He would assess that he had worked hard and deserved to be happy. But didn't she, too? She loathed all the players in the twisted game, all the ones who had stolen what was hers. It all belonged to her. And now this bitch had taken the one thing she had left—her child. She rocked the child as if she owned the precious gift. As if it had been hers to hold all along. Bitch. She didn't deserve that title. The Watcher would reclaim what belonged to her—if it killed her.

Eight.

Patience had always been her strongest virtue, even in the toughest times. She was okay with watching, with waiting. And so, she had waited. Waited for her to crack. Waited to do research, to find the answers she needed. She did her research and took her time. She knew exactly when and where to call home after she had to leave her last one. Oakwood had to be her next stopping point because, well, what other choice did she have?

Seven.

Crows cursed above her head as if the heavens themselves were sending an omen. She'd never been superstitious, though, and she no longer believed in signs. Perhaps that part of her was broken. Perhaps it always was.

She'd forced her way to the back of the forest, dark and brooding with an ominous mist. She'd settled in between the trees where, in actuality, she always felt at home. She inhaled the earthy air and exhaled freedom. She would stay as long as it took. She wouldn't leave the woods until she reclaimed what was hers. What had always been hers.

Rose thought she could move in on her territory and take her baby in the crook of her arm. She thought she could just take over and claim ignorance, pretend the past didn't matter. But the Watcher laid claim to her possessions long before Rose could even consider doing such a thing. She would not let some sad twat lay claim to what would always be hers.

Six.

She'd worn the expensive perfume that made her feel sexy. She'd wriggled into the black dress that hugged her in all the right ways. And now, standing before him, she could see it had worked. She'd snagged him, this perfect man to complement her life, her choices, her ways. He was everything to her. And he was looking at her in a way that suggested he felt the same.

It was a full moon, something her mother had always been attuned to note. Her mother used to put out the crystals and drink the moon water, anything to bring good luck for a better future. She thought it would bring them prosperity. But the Watcher knew you couldn't cast a spell to achieve happiness. You made it. You possessed it. You didn't let anyone usurp what was yours. That was the true spell to be cast—power in possession.

He leaned in now. "You're stunning," he said, and she thought it was just like him to use the perfect phrase, beautiful but unique. The word "stunning" floated in the clouds above her head as he took her mouth in his. As he made quick of connecting their hearts, their bodies, everything.

He possessed her. She let him.

But now, that ownership was severed and she was alone. All the fuck alone.

Five.

It would never be right again, she thought, reclining in the Scooby van's front seat and looking up at the full moon. There was no amount of crystals or good juju to make this all right now. Still, if she got the bitch out of the picture, if she slit her throat and let her blood run cold like a sacrificial lamb, maybe their love story wouldn't be so tainted.

Four.

Her arms cradled an imaginary baby. She thought of how it had been to hold that child for the first time. She saw her whole life in those baby blues. She closed her eyes now, knowing she would do anything to feel that fullness of life again.

Three.

Make her pay. Make her fucking pay. Blood on the door. It was just the beginning. Send her crazy. Make her insane. Watch her slowly spiral on her way to death...oh so slowly. Like a tortured mouse in a trap, its head bent at a funny angle. Pleasure was in the torture. That was the only way.

Two.

It was working. That homewrecker was losing it. She was screaming at Josh and growing distant with her husband. That wouldn't do for much longer. The Watcher gritted her teeth but smiled, knowing it was all working. It would be worth it soon.

One and three-quarters.

She stretched her body, releasing the tension threatening to explode, threating to implode in her chest. She couldn't wait very much longer. This was no longer a game. The boy, the man—they were depending on her, even if they didn't know it.

One and a half.

It was time. It was almost time. The thought intoxicated her, a sweet nectar flooding her poisoned veins.

One and a quarter...

Chapter Twenty-One
Rose
Wednesday Evening

She paced at the patio door as she stared out into the misty forest. Rain had fallen since she'd returned home, and the deck was slick and glassy. Her eyes focused, however, on the tree line. Beyond the thick patch of trees, she knew the asylum sat. She wondered if she were to step onto the deck and listen, really listen, she could hear the shrieks. She shuddered at the thought.

After the park, she'd made a stop at the library in town. She'd done some research on Oakwood, not even trying to hide what her motives were. She'd researched the archives and looked at the newspapers. She'd read the stories of the disappearances from the past, of the searches in the woods.

She perused the eerie tales that told her what she'd already come to know—the woods were dangerous. Oakwood was dangerous. People disappeared all the time. Why?

Whom could she trust now? The walls were closing in. She wondered if Cloey felt the same way. She wondered if Thad would believe her.

She took a deep breath, but no amount of therapeutic techniques would assuage her bubbling fear—danger awaited her.

And she didn't know if she would ever feel safe again.

"KEEP YOUR VOICE DOWN. The kids will hear," she hissed as they stood across from each other in the bedroom. She'd put Lilly in front of the television with her favorite cartoon playing. Joshua had, of course, rushed to his bedroom the second they came in. Thad had yanked Rose's arm, pulling her to the bedroom—but passion wasn't on his mind.

Her palms were sweating and her face felt so hot. She was afraid to be alone with him for the first time in their marriage, but she was more afraid of inflicting damage on their kids if they witnessed whatever was about to go down.

It was clear from the second he walked in the door after work that he was still riled up about their earlier exchange. She was, too, although she'd harped on the exchange significantly less than usual thanks to all the asylum talk and investigating. There were other dangers to consider, dangers that could hurt the children. For although Thad was in a volatile state of mind, he would never hurt their kids. That, she would swear her life on. She would swear Lilly's life on.

She swallowed as he gritted his teeth. His hand came down on the nightstand. "I should worry about the kids? Me? After what you've done?"

"Thad, please. Listen. I know what I did was wrong, and I'm sorry. But you have to listen to me. I don't think we're safe here. Someone is trying to hurt us, and I did some research today and—"

"Enough," he bellowed. "Fucking enough. I'm tired of your crazy blaming and obsessions. I thought this could be our fresh start, but I don't think you're capable of it. I tried. I've tried so hard, Rose, to help you through this. To help you see. But I can't do this anymore." His hands were in his pockets now, and melancholy plastered itself like a virus under his skin, painted in every nook and cranny for her to see. Her heart cracked. For the first time in six months, it hit her.

He was breaking, too. He wasn't the stolid, stalwartly man he wanted everyone to believe.

She took a step closer, squeezing shut the gap between them.

"I know. I know what it seems like. But it's different now. I promise. I did some research at the library, and there are all kinds of shady things here. The whole outsider vibe, it's real. People disappear here all the time. I don't think Cloey left on her own. I really think—"

His hand slammed down on the nightstand again, and she jumped, startled by the violent blow.

"I can't do this anymore. I can't. I've tried. I've tried to be the husband you needed, but I can't handle it anymore. I'm trying to glue this family together, and you're tearing us apart? Can't you see?"

He turned from her, and she felt her hand instinctually grab for him. It found nothing but thin air. It wisped between her fingers and, like a dissipating puff of smoke, was gone.

Hope was gone.

He leaned on the window sill. For a moment, she hoped the creature of the legends, the lunatics from the asylum, the watcher from the woods—any of them, really—would appear, would help him see she wasn't crazy or delusional. She wanted them to be thrown together in tragedy, not tossed apart. She wanted him to love her again.

She hated desperate women. She hated how needy Jade had been. She'd scoffed at her, telling herself she'd never become that. Time shifted everything, though.

He stared out the window, and Rose stared at his back.

"Apparently, I do marry fucking psychos. You're all nuts. You're all fucking nuts," he whispered, turning to her now. His eyes were alight with fire, but not the kind she once loved. It was an uncontrollable flame that would incinerate her if she left it.

Maybe Jade wasn't the crazy one after all, she thought, as his hands shook sadistically and he ripped at his own hair. She imagined him pulling out entire chunks, tossing them to the floor in a bloodied mess.

She understood that feeling. She wanted to tell him, but she figured he already knew.

He left then, brushing by her like she was a specter. She felt like one, the remnants of a woman he used to know. She wondered if they'd ever know each other again, truly.

Life had shifted, but the memories had not.

Chapter Twenty-Two

Rose

The past

It was pitch black in the alley when she burst through the private, employee-only back door and spilled into the stony pathway. Breathless, she inhaled the harbor's air, rushing to the railing to lean on it and look out into the still water. Vomit swelled in her throat, but she swallowed it back down. The space, the air—it all felt better out here, despite her spinning head.

They'd insisted this was a good idea. Some group of friends she had.

As her heart stopped racing, she settled into a normal breathing pattern. Their hearts had been in the right place. Still, this wasn't her scene. She plucked the ridiculous birthday crown they'd put on her head and chucked it into the water. She was proud of herself—she hadn't cried. Even when she saw him across the pulsating room of drunk dancers, hanging on the skinny blonde girl. She'd held her composure, excusing herself to the bathroom. And then, she'd bolted, her head whirling with nausea and heartbreak.

It was the past, she told herself. Life was good. She was working at a new salon and would be opening her own eventually if all went well. She had a group of amazing friends from beauty school who had made sure she didn't sulk too long in her dingy apartment after Brian left her. They'd patched her broken heart over the past few months. They'd reassured her she was on the path to something better. She didn't know about that. Even tonight, when they'd honked in the limo they'd rented out in front of her place and demanded she get in for a night out, she'd wanted to turn around and crawl right back under the covers, alone and wallowing. She wanted to shut out the world. It was all dismal and glassy, just like the waters in the harbor. She wrapped her arms around her scantily clad top, elbows on the railing.

She wanted nothing more than to disappear sometimes.

The club's music grew deafeningly loud again as the door behind her swang open. She jumped, turning to see whether another employee or a serial killer was popping through the door. To her surprise, it seemed like neither.

He was overdressed for a place like this, stuffy looking in a pressed suit. His tie was still snuggly around his neck, a dark shade of something undetectable in the night air. He didn't seem to notice her, rushing straight for the railing just as she had. He breathed heavily for a moment, running a hand through his hair. Finally, when the silence enveloped him as it had her, he turned to look at her.

She smiled at him. "Peaceful out here, huh?"

He nodded, silent but warm somehow. He looked back out at the harbor but quickly averted his eyes to the left, to the right, as if he were looking for something.

"Maybe I'm getting old, but it's too much in there. How does anyone find this fun?" he asked, and she calmed at the connection. She'd thought the same.

"I don't know. It's too sweaty in there. It's just too much."

"So, are you here with friends or a significant other?" he asked, turning sideways to the harbor so he could have a better visual. Even in the peaceful night, he seemed edgy somehow. His fingers tapped out a rhythm on the railing. She eyed him, her instincts telling her she should go back inside. She didn't know him, and out here, there were no witnesses. Still, something in the tenor of his voice, in his confident stance—it didn't scream danger. She moved closer to him, a significant gap still existing between them.

"Friends. It's my birthday, so they brought me out."

"Happy birthday," he said, smiling.

"Thanks. I'd rather be home, though. Is that lame? Maybe I'm getting old, too."

He shook his head. *"You don't look anywhere near the descriptor of old."*

"In fairness, it's pitch black out here."

Silence permeated between the strangers again, but she didn't mind. She didn't feel the need to rush back in or to fill the emptiness. They stared out at the harbor, the clouds floating by and blocking out select stars from time to time.

"So what are you doing out here? Besides the fact that it's too sweaty in there?" she finally asked.

He sighed. *"It's complicated. My friends brought me out, too. A post-divorce party of sorts. Their hearts were in the right place, too, but I'm just not feeling it."* He admitted the words without hesitation. She liked his vulnerability.

"Do you still love her?" she asked. After the words were out, she thought she should apologize. He was a stranger, for God's sake. She didn't even know his name. What business of hers was it?

"No. God no," he immediately answered. He looked at her now, taking a step closer to her as well. She stared at him, and even in the darkness, she could see the pain in his eyes. "We've been done for a long time. You know the story. Married young, right out of high school. Had a baby. Drifted apart. But, well, it's more than that. She's always been—unstable. Frightening in recent years. And now that we're divorced, well, things are downright disastrous."

"I'm sorry," she said.

"No, I'm sorry. I didn't mean to dump all that on you." He turned again as if examining the alley, as if he expected the boogie monster to hop out at any minute.

"You seem anxious," she observed.

He pinched the bridge of his nose and exhaled. "Yes. Well, things have been rough. Let's just say she hasn't really been that interested in letting me go."

She shook her head. She thought she had it bad with Brian, but he just had moved on. Looking at the confident, strong man before her, she realized that if he felt vulnerable, there must be something truly frightening to the woman he'd left.

"What about you? Do you have someone in there waiting for you?" he asked.

She raised an eyebrow, and the man put his hands out.

"Wow, I'm really fucking all this up. That sounded super creepy. I just mean, we've been talking a lot about me, and I was wondering about you."

She grinned. "It's okay. I figure if you wanted to dump my body in the harbor, you'd have done it by now. No, there's no one. I mean, there's one of my exes in there, which is why I made my escape. He broke up with me two months ago, and now he's in there grinding on some girl like our two-year relationship never existed. I don't want it to bother me, but it does."

The man nodded, and then turned and leaned back on the railing, perhaps succumbing his anxious fears to the night sky.

"Love sucks, huh?" he asked.

She grinned. "It does. But I guess I still believe it could be out there, you know?"

"Hopeless romantic, then," he teased.

"More like cautiously ambitious romantic wannabe."

"That's a mouthful. Sounds like a song or something," he replied.

"A depressing one."

"Well, you probably should get back to your friends," he murmured, turning to face her. With her eyes adjusted in the darkness, she realized he looked more than just powerful in the suit. He was strong and built, his jawline sharp. She found herself biting her lip and then stopped herself. The guy just got divorced and was dealing with some stalker ex-wife. She needed to tone it down.

"And you to yours," she replied. But neither made a move.

The man put his hands in his pockets and exhaled. "Look, I know this is weird because we literally met in a back alley a few minutes ago. And I know you don't know me, so it's okay if you say no. But there's a little coffee shop down the block that is much more my scene. What do you say we both text our friends a "thanks but no thanks" and head over for some coffee? Talk a little bit more about the trials and tribulations of love or talk about the weather for all I care. Just so there isn't thumping music."

"And gyrating exes," she added, smiling. "Okay. But on one condition."

He nodded, waiting for her to ask.

"Tell me your name. That way if you are a murderer, my friends will know who to look for."

He smiled. "Thad Taylor."

She extended a hand. He took it with his and shook it, firmly and warmly.

"Rose Denzel," she replied.

He didn't let go of her hand. Instead, he twirled her playfully, not at all to the beat of the bumping bass coming from the club. She laughed and then took his arm as he led her down the back alley to the coffee shop.

She noticed he didn't look over his shoulder once on the way to the coffee shop, which made her smile inside.

Chapter Twenty-Three
Rose
Thursday Morning

She hated it when the dreams tousled her like a feather at sea. They came without warning, sometimes fast, sometimes tepid stories that morphed into the horrors of that night. There was always the same detail, though. The red braids torn out, floating in a puddle of blood. And then there was the noise, the shriek of Hades amplified to a soul-piercing level.

They scared her.

They were fake, though. Nothing like that could happen she reminded herself. That morning, when the dream roused her, she immediately went to Lilly's bed to make sure. She slept there soundly in her yellow dress. Always in yellow. It was so hard to get her out of it. She sucked her thumb, and even from the doorway, Rose smiled at the warmth radiating from her angelic girl.

She'd sighed and put the coffee on. It was too early to tackle anything but too late to go back to bed. Her head raged with pain, both from the dreams and from the night before. She hated sleeping by him after those horrid things he'd said. She'd wanted to leave, to take the kids and go. But she had stayed. Why? Weakness? Dependence? She busied her hands with a rag on the counter and looked out the window.

It was silent, the trees blowing softly in a light wind. It looked peaceful, even without the sunlight up. But she thought about the secrets out there, hidden in the forest. She thought about the things she'd read, about the horrors lurking. Her morbid curiosity got the better of her.

She walked onto the deck after slowly, carefully sliding the door open. She glanced to the right, half expecting some creature or villain to be awaiting her blood. There was nothing. It had rained the night before, and a soft glaze of reflective water pooled on the uneven portions of the deck. She trudged through them, barefoot, chilling but feeling alive.

An owl hooted in the distance, an unsettling, freight train chanting in the blackness. She was alone, the house still asleep. How easily she could disappear, just like the others. Perhaps some of them had wanted to. She understood that, the desire to cut all ties and run into the forest, a woman of the woods and not of this painful society. She gripped the railing as if she could hold herself back.

She held her breath for a moment, wanting to take in all the sounds. The owl had quieted, and there was a stillness about her as if even nature had sensed something was amiss. Her heart sped up, and she told herself she was crazy. But then, no, no she wasn't. She heard it.

A whistle. An abrasive note alternating with another.

A bird, perhaps? But in the darkness?

She braced herself, thinking about going in.

She leaned toward the woods as if she could hear the words better.

And then, she couldn't be sure, but as she peered into the tree line, she swore she saw red. Bright red, glowing oddly in the darkness. And before she could dash back inside, she knew what she heard.

A flat voice chanting just above the forest white noise.

You're dead.

She ran inside to wake her husband, running right past her daughter's bedroom. There was no more peaceful sleep to be had.

He had to believe her now. He had to. Otherwise, she knew she was a dead woman.

Chapter Twenty-Four

Rose

Thursday Morning

How could you simultaneously fucking hate someone and worship them? How could your heart literally split in two, half blackened to the thought of him and half still pulsing with his?

She rocked herself on the couch, holding the doll, her comfort object now. Tears fell onto the doll's soft, wispy hair.

He didn't believe her. She was here, in this house, with a monster out there, and he didn't believe her. After everything, he still never believed her.

He hadn't believed her when she'd told him about her after the incident.

He had told her she was going mad from the trauma. He told her that now, too.

He'd placated her like some sad, helpless heroine in an 1800s novel then.

This morning, when she'd woken him up in hysterics about a voice in the forest, he'd done something worse: he'd threatened to get her help, real help. She knew what that meant. She could almost hear the asylum's cries from here. Was that what he'd brought her here for? Her mind wrapped around the possibility that suddenly made so much effortless sense. And then, after dropping that conversation, he'd left for work, leaving her to fend for herself. Of course, he did.

Rocking back and forth, her hands stroked the doll's hair. He didn't believe her. He wasn't on her side. Perhaps he never was. She pulled the doll away from her to get a better look, her fingers tracing the word Evette on its leg. Why there? What did it mean? And why did she leave it behind?

The photo album in the attic. She'd thumbed through it, thinking nothing of it. But so much had changed in so little time. Maybe there was more to this house, to this story. Maybe they just wanted her to think Cloey was a bad person. Maybe Thad, the town, they were all working together. Maybe she shouldn't trust any of them at all.

She was suddenly sure of it all. She knew that the answers, too, could be found up there, in that attic in the album. She left a clue. That's what she did. This Cloey woman was the only one who could be trusted, she realized. She put the doll down, safely tucked in the corner of the couch. She kissed her sweet forehead.

"I'll be right back, Noodle." She giggled a bit. That was her name for Lilly, after all. How ridiculous.

And then she crawled up the stairs to do some more searching. She'd always liked clue hunts—but this time, her life depended on it. The stakes had never been so damn high.

SHE PEEKED BACK THROUGH the album, picture after picture of Evette smiling in different poses. Rose found herself admiring the sweet baby's photos. She pulled a few out to put downstairs. They cheered her. She got a hold of herself quickly, though. She needed to see what she could find. She needed to solve the mystery somehow, against all odds, if she wanted to secure her life. Their life. Lilly's life. That was all that mattered now.

She looked through every page for a clue, for a hint. She pulled a few photos out to see if they contained a message or at least dates. Nothing. She turned up nothing. She shoved the album back in the box and gave it a little kick, frustrated that the filthy attic and risk of seeing a rat had led her no closer to her goals. She sat back, having previously been propped up on her knees. She glanced around the crawlspace, wondering what Cloey went through when she hid this stuff up here. Was she utterly alone? Trying to protect her own child? What drove her away?

She rubbed her face with her gritty hands and was about to go back down, when her eyes landed on something she'd missed before. A box, smaller this time, tucked near the edge of the attic. It was a black, metal box. Nondescript, it had blended in with the attic's drudgery. Now, though, her eyes adjusted and her mission clear, she'd spotted it as if she was meant to.

She crawled on her hands and knees across the splintery floor, immune to the pain of the jagged edges as she reached for the box. The lid popped off when she pulled on the metal handle. There was no lock. Cloey must've felt confident no one would find this—or perhaps she'd meant for someone to, Rose considered with a fresh perspective.

The lid popped off. Her fingers were trembling, unable to root through the items fast enough. On top, a Ziplock baggy covered the items below. She plucked it from the treasure chest and held it up to the dim light streaming through the gritty, tiny window. She realized at once, with some iciness, what was inside.

Locks of hair. Several filling the bag. And then, she realized, that the blackish substance dried to the bottom of the bag was blood, as if some of the hunks of hair had been ripped from the root. These were not lockets of a precious child's hair preserved by a mother's love, she recognized, as she tossed the bag to the floor with a tiny gasp.

There was a piece of paper folded beneath the baggie, a long, detailed number that started with a B, if her squinting eyes discerned it correctly. Other relics of the stranger's life filled the box. Two rings, gold in color, an envelope of cash, a few necklaces. She pawed them all aside. They were not what she needed.

Her hand reached into the box more hesitantly now, fear shielding her determination. Slowly, carefully, she reached in, deciding to root to the very bottom as bravery usurped her terror. Her fingers traced a glossy, plastic surface. When she pulled it from the ruins of whatever life Cloey had left behind, she gasped again, this time in twisted, tainted relief.

Chapter Twenty-Five

Rose

Thursday Morning

She couldn't get down the stairs fast enough, hope alight in her heart for the first time in a long while. Her hands clung to the item like it was the Holy Grail, the golden chalice of salvation. For her, it might be.

She could barely breathe when she got to her laptop and typed the name in the search bar.

Evette Harding.

Not Cloey Fountain. Evette Harding. That was who had lived in the house before her. She'd used an alias, so no wonder Rose hadn't been able to find much on her. She'd tucked away her real life. Now, the question was: why?

Rose sat the glossy license to the right of the computer, staring into the eyes of the black-haired woman in the picture. The entire town had commented on how Rose's red hair was just like Cloey's. So clearly Evette had gone to extreme lengths to disguise herself. And as the search bar populated results that Rose could barely read fast enough, her jaw dropped.

She knew why. She now knew why.

And suddenly, more than ever, she didn't feel safe at all. She got up to make sure the door was locked. Tears welled, confusion whirring. The town had been right after all. They'd just gotten the name wrong and the story.

They'd sensed Cloey Fountain wasn't who she said she was, wasn't some sweet, innocent red head who carried around a doll. Still, there was something quite wrong with her. Something quite wrong indeed.

Rose rocked on the couch, trying to piece it together, trying to sort it out.

For if Evette Harding, as the newspaper article suggested, was a wanted woman who had murdered her husband in cold blood, what would she do to the people living with her belongings? And why hadn't she come back already?

She thought about the blood on the door, the beheaded animals. She thought about all the times she felt watched out on the deck.

Evette Harding was waiting to strike. She'd been patient the past few days, given her a warning. But Rose and Thad hadn't listened. They'd stayed in the house. Rose's blood turned cold as she realized she'd even committed what Evette must consider the ultimate crime—she'd stolen her sweet doll. Hell, the woman carved her own name on the thing's leg. Suddenly, the doll wasn't a comfort or a warmth. It was something to be rid of.

She needed to show Thad. She needed to convince him to leave. They weren't safe here. They just weren't. It wasn't madness or grief or anything else. It was the truth—this place was dangerous. She had evidence now to show him. Her real license in the back. Evette. She sent him a text.

Call me. Urgent.

She paced for a moment, trying to catch her breath. Yes, she knew what she needed to do. She wasn't some helpless woman who needed saved. She would do her own saving today. Mother to mother, she knew what Evette needed.

She took another deep breath to calm her shaking hands, shoved her phone in her pocket along with the license, and headed out to make her family safe. She could finally do something to make them safe. She had to at least try.

Chapter Twenty-Six

Rose

Thursday Late Morning

She stood before the towering trees, the shadowed darkness with open arms and a guarded heart. She thought of the woman on the license, the murderer who once lived in the house. She thought of the woman who had been watching, perhaps just waiting for her prized possession back.

She set down the album, the sweet, angelic doll on top.

"I'm sorry," she whispered, for who, she didn't know. Monsters did live in those woods. But they lived all around them too. And who knew what monsters Evette Harding had faced before she became one herself.

She walked away from the sacrificial lamb, the white flag, and turned her back to the woods. Her mind ran awry with images of a knife in her back, of blood spewing. It was a tense few steps, but she cleared it just fine.

She stood on the deck, watching, but knew she wouldn't come with her there. She went back inside. She texted Thad again, the fifth time. He still did not answer.

Knights were only good when the sun was shining. She'd learned that long ago.

She went out the front door, wary and feeling empty. She already missed having the doll with her. She would have to go on without the comfort object again. She walked on and got the bus, heading to her final stop.

"I'm sorry," she whispered again, as she walked through the foreboding building.

She had to do whatever it took.

Chapter Twenty-Seven

Rose

Thursday Afternoon

She told herself to quiet her tapping foot as she sat on the rigid chair in the lackluster waiting area. The license burned a hole in her pocket, scalding her already fragile skin. She looked down at her phone. Still no response. Perhaps that bridge was severed for good. She shuddered but stilled her cracking heart. She would have to deal with that later.

She'd been in the police station for at least forty-five minutes now, waiting to speak with the officers. The secretary had been nosy but complacent when she'd told her she had important information and was potentially in danger. She'd snapped her gum and wordlessly gestured toward the lone, tan chair in the corner. She continued her loud, gossipy conversation on the phone, in no real hurry to usher Rose back to the officers, her real knights in this situation if all went well. So she'd waited. She'd practiced her story. She'd waited some more.

She texted Thad several times. He'd left her on read. The woman who cried wolf, he must have labeled her, as he returned to his lattes and talks of awnings. She'd dialed the work number in an effort to get to him, to convince him she wasn't crazy or lying. She knew he was grieving in his own way, and that perhaps this was all too much for him, too, even if he wouldn't admit it. The secretary, though had told her surprising news.

He was gone. Out of town, on the road. He was expected back later that evening. She was peeved. He hadn't even told her. What about the kids? She supposed they would take the bus. Again, not something to worry about now.

So she'd waited on the last, trivial hope she had—the police. They would hear her story and finally validate her. Perhaps they'd search her house, the woods. They'd set up patrols to keep her and the family safe. She'd be lauded as a hero in town instead of the outsider. Maybe with the peace that would come from it all, Thad would remember why it had to be this way. He'd see her for the strong, capable woman she was again.

The officer emerged from his closet-like office and made glaring eye contact with her. She offered a weak smile and wave. He wordlessly ambled to the coffee pot chugging away in the corner of the front area and poured himself a generous cup. After a long, dramatic groan and stretch from him, he walked back to his office.

"You. In the waiting room. Come on back."

She stood from her chair as if she were just picked for a morbid gameshow, anxious to run down the aisle and see what fate awaited her.

SHE TOLD HER STORY. She showed him the license. He tried to stay neutral, but it was clear that when she mentioned Cloey Fountain, his attention perked up. He studied the license with clear intrigue. He cleared his throat, asking a few questions as she told of the bloodied words on the door, the animals, the feeling of being watched.

And when she was done, she waited for him to leap into action. A heavy anchor lifted from deep within. She felt freer, safer, more hopeful.

And then it all came crashing down.

"Well, thanks, Ms. Taylor. I'll certainly look into all this." He tucked the license in a folder with the few notes he'd taken and shoved it in his desk.

"You did hear the part about the warrant, right? The murder?" she asked, stunned at his calm demeanor. She'd just dropped a bombshell that would rock the town.

"I did. I heard you quite well. Listen, you have nothing to worry about, I assure you. Ms. Fountain or Ms. Harding, as you suggest, isn't going to hurt you."

A creeping sensation slipped into her throat, her chest, her blood. The look in the officer's eyes was cold, deadened almost. The slightly perceptible grin on his face hinted at a malevolence not typically desired in an officer of the law but perhaps the side effect of living a life in law enforcement.

She tried to shake the feeling. "I'm just concerned for my family. After the bloody displays, I just feel very threatened."

He sighed. "We'll send an officer to check the woods again, okay?" His eyes softened in a forced display of empathy, but she'd seen that look so many times before. So many of them had plastered it on their faces back in her old town to cover the truth written on their faces—the accusations against her and her incompetence.

She had been an outsider then, changed from beloved business owner to sitting on the fringes. No one had cared. She was an outsider now, the officer's brown eyes reminded her despite his weak efforts. She knew that already, though. She'd known that from the first day.

God, did she know that. She got up to leave. She was on her own. Again.

"Ms. Taylor?" the officer asked when she was at the door. She turned to look at him. He was now standing at his desk. "We're not going to have any issues over this, are we? I would hate to think someone new to town would come in and stir things."

"And how would I do that?"

He shrugged. "Making a spectacle out of this. Calling other police departments when we are more than capable of handling it here ourselves."

His left hand traveled to a very blatantly challenging position—it rested on his gun.

Her stomach sank, but she did her best to stand straight and proud.

"Of course, not, Officer. I wouldn't dream of it," she replied. She was many things. She wasn't many things.

She was not, though, a fool.

Chapter Twenty-Eight
The Watcher
Thursday Afternoon

Blood boiled in her veins as she clenched her jaw. It would be laughable if it didn't piss her off so much. The doll sat on the album, a sick and twisted offering—to what? A God that didn't care about her? To a woman who didn't, either? Did she really think this made up for it all, absolved her from her reckless sins?

The Watcher picked up the items and took them back to the van. It wouldn't do to have her out in the cold, after all, for anyone to find. She was smarter than that, of course. And the woman was doing a damned good job at setting herself to be written off as suicidal and crazy. Even Thad was clearly sick of her craziness. He was barely home, and she'd heard the raised voices, even from the tree line.

She was curious about one thing—where she was going. She'd been shaking like a leaf when she dropped the offering of items with a pathetic apology into the forest. But then, she'd vanished, walking purposefully out the front door although frequently looking over her shoulder. The Watcher had smiled at that. It felt so luxurious to have some power over her. She'd almost forgotten what that felt like.

She waited now, for the return. For the finale. For the denouement no one expected. No one but her. It was time to play, to finish their story—so she could begin hers anew.

She sat in the van now and pulled out the burner phone. She wanted so badly to text him, to tell him she still loved him. It was pointless, though. Their story was dead, had been dead. She would have to write her own epilogue—and it would be a bloody one.

She typed in the number and sent the text. She smiled, picturing Rose's face as she read the eerie words.

It had started. The game had begun. It would all be finished.

Tonight.

Chapter Twenty-Nine
Rose
Thursday Afternoon

A lone rider sat at the back of the bus, a teenager clinging to a backpack with an unlit cigarette in his hand. She made eye contact with him before claiming a seat a respectable distance away. Frustration, fear, horror—it all loomed within her, a toxic soup poisoning her every thought. Total despair threatened to usurp her completely, but she clung to her only saving grace—herself. She would sort it out, figure out how to save them. Even if it meant doing the unthinkable and leaving with Lilly, she would protect her from whatever outside force there was. She would protect them both from everyone, the two of them against the world.

For now, she needed to get home and keep an eye out. She needed to give Thad a chance to see things for what they were. It would be easier with him on her side. He had to know. He had to be able to see through the grief, to strengthen up once more for their family.

Her phone buzzed, and she anxiously pulled it from her pocket, hoping to see the familiar pet name she had for her husband on the screen. Instead, a text message from an unfamiliar number lit up her phone. She read the text once, twice, three times. The kid in the back of the bus ambled past her, singing loudly to a song she didn't know. Her head whirled around, the words on the screen making her realize she wasn't crazy. Danger was lurking, right around the corner. And perhaps she'd been wrong about the who or the what.

She looked at the words:

You won't get away with it. Just when you think I've quit, when you think I'm not there to watch you with him anymore, I'll surprise you. I'll bring your worst nightmares to reality. You think what happened to you was bad? It can get worse. No one messes with my child, especially not a slut like you.

Evette Harding was capable of horrid things. She could be the one watching. But there was someone else who spoke in that cadence, who would say those things.

When she got to the stop near their house, Rose rushed off the bus and ran for the door. She waited at the kitchen table, constantly tapping, constantly looking about, as she waited for the one person who could help her deduce who was behind it.

If only he would be willing to step up to the task. For he did not know all that had transpired in those early days. He didn't know what kind of woman she really was.

Chapter Thirty
Rose
The Past

Maybe he would believe her now. Maybe he would really believe her now.

He was on the phone with the police in the living room as she hovered over the bathroom sink, leaning deep into the shiny, white basin. Her shaking hands reached up to touch her now-spiky hair, the clump that had been removed like a piece of her own presence vanished. Slowly, oh-so-tenderly, she raised her eyes to glance in the mirror. Her eyes were puffy from tears, her pallor gray. The mascara she'd worn last night dribbled down her cheeks, underlining the redness plastered on her face.

She was not the same now.

She thought she should go out to the living room and help him handle it. Joshua had been sent to the neighbor's house across the street, the sweet, elderly lady entertaining him with tea and stories of her cat, Amos. They hadn't wanted him to hear about what his mother had done. She knew she should brave up and go out there. Thad, after all, couldn't be taking this well. It could've been worse.

So much worse. He had to know that. In the depths of denial, he had to know that Jade hadn't just wanted to stop at cutting her hair.

Rose sat on the lid of the toilet, one hand instinctually rubbing her stomach. She waited until she felt the familiar kick to reassure herself that she was still in there, that she wasn't harmed. If the baby had been harmed, Rose didn't know what she'd have done.

She leaned back now, drained from the afternoon's events.

It had started with a trip home from prenatal yoga. Thad was at work, and Joshua was at daycare. Everything was normal, a typical Tuesday. The day glimmered with hope. Rose breathed in the spring air. She was a newlywed with a baby on the way. A girl, just like she always wanted. She had everything she could want—the man of her dreams, plans for a new salon she would run after the baby was born, and most of all, hope. Peace. Happiness. Except for the single black stain threating to blot out all her joy.

Jade.

Rose understood why Jade was pissed. In a way, Rose had walked away with what Jade probably thought was her life. It didn't matter that Jade had made her bed, that her relationship with Thad was well over the night Rose had met him. It didn't matter to women like her. All she saw was a stepmother taking her place in her son's life, and a woman taking her place in her ex-husband's bed.

So when Thad married Rose and broke the news gently to Jade, that's when the eerie, stalkerish behavior switched from targeting him to targeting her.

There had been so many encounters. Rose found herself always watching over her shoulder, keys in her hands anytime she went out alone. She would feel a presence when she left the bakery, sense someone rushing away when she turned to look at the bushes after her appointments. She'd told Thad, but he'd written it off. She felt uneasy, though. She'd finally convinced to have a new security system installed the next week just so she could actually sleep.

"Jade has calmed down. Honestly. She knows I've moved on. She wouldn't hurt you because she wouldn't risk losing Joshua," he'd argued.

It wasn't enough to convince her, though.

Still, that morning, she'd breathed in the sunshine air and felt like, for the first time, things were okay. She didn't feel the need to look over her shoulder. She walked with a little more lilt in her gait, a little more confidence in her view of the world. They were turning a corner.

She'd come home, made herself a sandwich, and relaxed into a luxurious afternoon of nothing to do. She decided to take a shower before Thad came home. Wandering into the bathroom, stretching her neck like a lethargic cat, she'd closed the door behind her. She'd walked over to the shower curtain and peeled it back.

And then, she screamed in terror as she jumped back. For with crazed eyes and a witch's cackle, Jade had leaped out of the tub, a pair of scissors in her hand.

Rose had screamed and struggled, shoving at the woman. She needed to protect herself, not for her own life, but for her baby. She grunted and shoved as Jade laughed and taunted her.

"Did you think you could have him?" she'd screamed, the scissors snapping at her.

She moved her head to avoid being stabbed. Jade sheared off a clump of her long, red hair. Rose kept fighting.

"Stop, please. Stop," she pleaded, her arms shaking against Jade's strength fueled by vehemence.

"You'll pay, bitch. You'll pay."

Rose looked into the eyes of her assailant. They were wild and unstable. She was wild and unstable. She was going to die. She was for sure going to die.

"Think of Joshua," Rose said, the only thing that came to mind.

A pause. A look came over Jade. The scissors, poised in the air, lowered slightly. Tears started to well.

"Shit," the monster whispered. "Shit," she said.

And just like that, she'd walked out of the room, Rose trembling against the wall. Rose shut the bathroom door behind her and locked in, sobs racking her body. She made herself be quiet as she listened. Footsteps. Crying. The clicking of the door. She was gone.

She ran to the kitchen and grabbed her phone. Her fingers dialed Thad, even though she knew she should call the cops.

And just like that, it was over. A chunk of hair missing. The fake sense of safety lost.

It was over, but never completely.

"SHE KILLED THE NEIGHBOR'S cat. You told me yourself," she argued in the kitchen. The police were on their way, and they didn't have much time, Thad had told her. She stood in front of him. He was pacing. He didn't look well.

"It was an accident. She didn't mean to hit the cat," he replied, as if that were the point.

"Then why did you tell me she did?" Anger surged through her. Were they really arguing this point now.

"Listen, Rose. Please. Jade was never perfect. Ever. It was probably why I fell in love with her. I saw a chance to help her."

"Is that what you see in me? A pity case? A sad girl who needs saving?" She stomped her feet, more tears brimming in her eyes. She'd thought she'd cried all the tears she could.

"You're strong and independent. You're nothing like her. You're not—"

"Crazy? Psychotic? An attempted murderer? Why do you want to let her go? Why are you protecting her?" She screamed, fighting the urge to pound on his chest with her fists as he stood there, arms splayed out in a forgiving gesture.

He sighed, pinching the bridge of his nose between his thumb and forefinger. "It's complicated."

"No, it's not. No, it's fucking not. She tried to kill me. And you're defending her."

He looked up at her. "I'm not. If I thought for a minute she would actually do it, I'd kill her myself. It's just—since the divorce, it's been hard for her. I was her rock. Always. And without me there to keep her on her meds—"

"She's not your mother," Rose said, a line he hated but needed to hear. "Just because you couldn't save your mother doesn't mean you have to be the hero for Jade. She makes her own choices. And this one was wrong, depression or not."

He stepped forward, reaching for her hand. She resisted, but his pleading eyes always got her. She offered her hand to him, and he kissed it softly. Her heartbeat calmed.

"Listen. I know what she did was awful. But please. Trust me. She has done some shady stuff. But she isn't a murderer. She just needs help. And she's Josh's mother. Think about how he would feel if she was locked away for good? Certainly, she needs to pay for what she's done. But I think we can come to an agreement."

"If we press charges, you could get full custody."

"And as selfishly as I want that, I know for Josh, that's not what's best. He loves her. I can't be the one to separate them. I know what it's like to not have a parent."

Rose felt her hand again go to her stomach. She could imagine that.

"Jade just feels like we took Josh away since we have partial custody. She feels like you're taking over because he likes you better. What she did was awful, but she's not a wicked person. Please, all I'm asking is for a chance. Let's give her a chance to set it right. To go to therapy. To go to placement for a while. To prove to us she's sorry and serious."

The door bell rang. The police had arrived. She had to make a decision of what she would say, how much she would tell. She looked into his eyes, the man she loved, the man she vowed to do anything for. She saw the hurt, the pleading, the struggle. And so she took a breath.

She hadn't been hurt.

Thad would protect her. Right?

Maybe Jade did just need help. She imagined what she would do if someone tried to step into her motherly shoes.

She would do anything for her child, she knew. Anything.

And so, she stood as Thad answered the door. She knew what she had to do.

Chapter Thirty-One
Rose
Thursday Afternoon

The years after were tenuous at best although relatively safe. Jade had been checked into a placement where she got counseling and help for a slew of issues that had gone untreated. Rose and Thad continued their lives, welcoming baby Lilly and navigating the life of two families for Joshua. Things were normal, as much as they could be. However, Rose always saw Jade with a wary eye. She could never be trusted, even when she seemed calmer, better. Oftentimes, randomly, Rose would get the feeling someone was watching her still, but Thad dismissed it as paranoia. Rose was never convinced.

All was well. Until it wasn't. Until that day she wouldn't think about. She twisted her fingers together, breathing deeply. It was fine. It wasn't real. Just a nightmare that shook her.

But when Thad planned the move, suggesting they needed space from that old town and all it contained, something slipped in Jade. There was no longer the calm, assuring presence when they dropped Josh off for his visitation weekends. There was a rage, a violent anger in her.

As Rose paced in the kitchen, waiting for her family to return, a lightbulb moment clicked. Things had been fine with Jade until they'd moved, until her son was taken to this new town, miles and miles and miles away. Her visitation would stay the same—but for a woman like Jade, the distance would certainly plague her. For any woman, Rose realized as she thought about sweet Lilly.

She'd been fooled. Or a fool. She'd gotten wrapped up in the Cloey/Evette fear mongering in town. She'd been lulled into a sleepy sense by the distance and let her guard down. She'd thought that Evette had been watching. But what would she have against her? Why would she engage in this cat and mouse game? She probably left town in a hurry after what happened. Why would she lurk about? If the doll was what she wanted, she would've just claimed it.

Rose sat on the couch, her head spinning with all the clues—and with the harsh reality that if she was right this time, things were way worse than she imagined.

SHE BARELY HAD TIME to ponder the new possibility when the door flung open and she jumped, her hand slapping to her chest. She turned to see the familiar chestnut hair and the scowl. Joshua slinked through the kitchen, avoidance his clear goal. He'd ridden the bus home, which always put him in a bad mood. Being alone with her also aggravated him. She didn't have time to worry about it.

"Joshua, I need you to do something important," she shouted. He did not stop in his tracks but continued walking, flinging belongings here and there as he beelined for his sanctuary.

"What?" he mumbled, barely audible over the dropping backpack and flung coat.

"Call your mother. I need you to call her and tell her you need her, ask how quickly she could be here."

He turned on his heel, his attention on her now. When he faced her, she could see the pure rage intertwined with his facial features.

"What the fuck?" he asked snarkily. She thought about correcting his language, but this was not the time for it.

"I need you to do this. It's important." She spoke in a commanding tone. He did not budge. A sneer plastered itself on his face as he shoved his hands in his pockets.

"You told me I couldn't," Joshua replied snarkily. She slammed her fists on the island, with gritted teeth.

"Dammit, this is important. Call your mother and see where she is. But don't tell her I want to know."

A standoff settled in, the two tensely eyeing each other from across the way. She stood a little taller. She needed him more than he needed her right now.

She won out, perhaps only because he wanted to talk to his mother. He pulled his phone out of his pocket and dialed the number. She listened carefully. If Jade was nearby and her son needed her, she would admit it in a heartbeat. She was a lot of things, but she wasn't a bad mother.

"Voicemail," he said after time had passed and no one answered. He hung up, shrugged, and went to his room.

Rose exhaled, wringing her hands. Could she have been wrong this whole time? Could Jade have been watching, waiting to strike? Maybe she was just more patient than she supposed. Perhaps these past years had been an act, the transformation of her attitude a smokescreen to protect her actual plan.

Rose walked to the patio doors and slid them cautiously. She peered out, feeling like she was sticking her neck in the guillotine but too curious, too engulfed in it all to let it slide. Her eyes scanned the ground as she leaned over the railing to look down.

And that was when her stomach fell.

The doll, the album—they were gone.

She flew back into the house.

"Watch your sister," she screamed out to Joshua, her feet not able to walk fast enough. It was over. She was done. Jade, Evette, whoever it was, she would solve it once and for all.

She armed herself with the best weapon she could grab, a kitchen knife. She dashed out onto the deck with wild abandon for her own safety. If they wouldn't believe her, she'd make them believe. She trounced down the deck stairs and headed into the unknown yet, paradoxically, known. She was out there, waiting for her. And Rose wouldn't let her win again. She wouldn't live under her reign of terror like she had before.

She plowed through the woods, deranged but focused. It was foolish, but she could no longer sit at her mercy. She had done that with Jade for all those years. She had sat by as she lurked in the boundaries of their marriage, outside their house, outside her business. She'd watched as the faulty fucking court system, her own husband, had protected the villain and had left her vulnerable. She'd watched as Jade kept leeching into their relationship.

No fucking more.

And if it wasn't Jade, if it was that Evette or Cloey or whoever the hell she was, she'd make her pay, too. She wasn't some weak little, grieving woman everyone thought. She could take care of herself.

I'll protect you.

I'll hold you.

I've got you.

Chapter Thirty-Two

Rose

Thursday Evening

Dear, don't go getting obsessed.

The words of her meddling mother, of Thad, of probably everyone chanted about her as she shoved through the forest. They thought she was worthless. Crazy. Written off.

She wasn't. She would fix this. She would solve it once and for all, lest she go mad waiting about for a resolution. For that was always the worst, wasn't it? The waiting. The not knowing. The sacrificial stance as you waited for the finale. Something was amiss. Someone was after her family. She couldn't protect them before. She *would* protect them now.

She tripped on a branch on the darkened path. Her feet dashed through the paths recklessly, the forest a tangled maze. It was futile, most likely. What were the chances she'd find the person? What was she thinking? A scream echoed in the air, a piercing cry that shook her deep within. She trudged on. On and on and on. A thought struck her, a dangerous thought perhaps.

The asylum. It wasn't far, if the woman at the park was to be believed. It was precariously close, in fact. And maybe if she got there, if she could get answers from them—maybe this wasn't about Jade or Cloey at all. Maybe something else was at play. Or perhaps Evette—

The stone building called to her, pulled her toward it, if for nothing else, then for curiosity's sake. She wanted to see the foreboding structure with her own eyes, feel that sinister vibe the woman had described. Perhaps if she saw it, something in her would know.

A mother always knows, they say. Maybe she should try.

Deeper into the forest she walked, every instinct telling her to go back. She paused for a moment to listen. She heard nothing, the piercing cry having stopped. She got a faint whiff of a putrid smell, a decaying fish tossed in kerosene smell. She rubbed her burning nose and turned to peer back. She couldn't see the house any longer. She thought of Joshua and Lilly, safe in the cocoon of her house. They would be safe there. She felt it in her blood. They were safe and that was all that mattered.

She would keep it that way. Her fingers gripped the knife's handle tighter. She moved forward, and although she didn't consciously know the way, she found that her feet seemed to.

For when she got to the iron wrought fence and peered into a forest of a different variety, she knew. Her heart knew.

The ground was blackened, hallowed.

She shivered, but the knife handle between her teeth, and began to climb the foreboding fence as if it was what she was always meant for.

Chapter Thirty-Three
The Watcher
Thursday Evening

The crazy bitch had lost her mind. It had finally happened. But the Watcher didn't care.

Stalking her prey from behind, slowly, meticulously, her hands rubbed the handle of her knife. It didn't matter that Rose was armed. She was too far gone to understand the danger, to know the truth—it was futile to fight. For the Watcher was adept at this sort of thing. She'd been practicing for this moment for her own life, she realized. It was all leading here, in a moment of glory.

The doll was tucked under her left armpit. She felt ridiculous bringing it, but there was something poetic in it. She enjoyed the thought of slaughtering Rose with the doll watching. Perhaps it was symbolism, perhaps it was madness. But something about the doll had called to her, and urged her to bring it along.

The bitch would die. Now. This wasn't how she'd pictured it happening. She'd pictured something quite different, intimate. Obvious even. But Rose was making it easy on her now. She watched as she climbed the iron gate, stumbling about like a newborn calf. It would be poetic justice but also disappointing if the moron slit her own throat with the knife in her teeth somehow. It would make the Watcher's job even easier—but also last satisfying.

No, since the first time she heard Rose's name, she'd dreamt of what it would be like to plunge a blade into her chest, to carve out the very beating heart that had stolen him from her.

Stolen both of them.

A mother's love is stronger than anything, they say. And she knew it to be true. For losing Thad had been difficult in its own way, devastating. Enraging.

But losing Joshua because this bitch couldn't keep it together: that was too much. That was too far.

She should have killed her when she first had the chance all those years ago. She should have fucking spilled her blood then in the shower and been done with it.

At least it wasn't too late. It was never too late.

She smiled as she waited for the perfect moment and then climbed the fence herself. She was much more graceful about it, of course. She'd always been in every way. When she landed, she checked on the doll. Not a faux hair on her head had been harmed.

She was a good mother, she knew.

Jade, the Watcher, was the best damned mother out there.

Chapter Thirty-Four

Rose

Thursday Evening

The forest near the asylum was dense, not just with shrubbery but also with a foreboding sensation that clung haphazardly in the air. Every breath in felt too dense, every breath out too shallow. She meandered through the forest maze, glimpses of the mammoth stone building ahead peering out. If she could talk to someone there, maybe she could find out if Evette had ended up there. It made sense—if the town wanted her to disappear, it seemed like this was the place for it. The building was its own island, clouded by a shroud of trees and mystery.

Before she could reach the lighted path in front of the asylum, though, footsteps sounded behind her. She turned around, ducking behind a tree in case guards were patrolling. She paused, holding her breath. Silence pervaded again.

Suddenly, it all rained down on her at once, the immense risk she was taking. Could she get inside somehow? Could she figure out if Evette was in there, at least, so she could rule her out? She looked over her shoulder, but the forest was so dense, it was impossible to see. There was an ominous feeling pounding in her chest, one indescribable. She heard whimpering from somewhere, and told herself it was just a rabbit. Still, it all felt impossible suddenly, a true fool's errand. She heard the rabbit whimper again. And then, she realized that rabbit whimpers didn't have that tone. She quelled the rising chaos in her veins and pushed forward.

Carefully, meticulously, she tiptoed through the foliage with the knife still in her hand. She crept on, breathless and weightless, determined to carry out her mission if it killed her.

A twig snapped behind her, an unmistakable clue she wasn't alone.

She whirled around again, and a scream rang out in the night as she saw the knife stabbing at her.

Finally, it all made sense.

Finally.

Chapter Thirty-Five
The Watcher
Thursday Night

The knife hurled toward the Watcher's target, but Rose moved just in time. The blade stuck into the tree bark, her hand jarred. She kicked her foot against the tree to pull it out as Rose stumbled to the ground. The doll slipped from Jade's hand, plummeting to the filthy Earth as she prepared to strike again.

She couldn't let her win. Her son's life depended on it. Josh needed her in his life, not this fake mother who was losing her mind. He needed to be close to her, not miles and miles away in this wasteland, this disconcerting town.

Rose plucked herself from the ground, wielding a knife, too.

Jade held her stance like she should have done all those years ago. Her feet rooted in the ground, she raised her knife. She was ready.

She had always been ready.

Footsteps echoed nearby, but Jade didn't have time to look. She dove forward, the knife again sailing toward its rightful target.

Chapter Thirty-Six
Thursday Night
Rose

P anic coursed in her veins as she picked herself off the ground. Her mind wanted to linger on the harsh reality that she'd missed the signs—it had been Jade all along. Of course it had been her. What had she been thinking? She'd gotten complacent over the years, and now she was going to die.

She wouldn't let her sweet child be alone. She wouldn't. Lilly needed her.

She dodged the knife coming at her once more. She emitted a wild scream as she tore toward Jade, her arms shaking with effort. They battled for a long moment, a war of two wills. And then, they both paused for an instant as a voice cried out.

"Mom?" a shaky male voice shrieked. Jade, perhaps out of instinct, turned to look, recognizing the voice that Rose also knew. But she didn't have time to wait. When Jade turned to look at Joshua, Rose struck. She took advantage, shoving her off balance and then, before she could think twice, plunging the knife into the woman's body. Once, twice, three times the blade tore through flesh as blood flew out. She stabbed and stabbed and stabbed until her blood flowed freely until her putrid green eyes faded away. Until Jade would never be able to leech into their marriage, into her life again. Sick bitch.

Screams echoed through the trees—the animalistic shriek still happening in the distance, shrieks from her own effort, a few screams from Jade before she went silent forever, and a male's cry as his hands eventually tore at her. Still, they were too late.

She struggled with him, a boy who, under this duress, had a man's strength to him. She battled and scratched, trying to calm him as Jade lay bloodied and dead.

Finally, she realized she had no choice. She needed to save her family. Her real family: Thad, Lilly, and her. Joshua didn't belong. He'd never belonged. Couldn't they understand that? He'd never loved her, and he'd never made space for her. There was only one thing she could do.

And so, the knife in her hand found the next target. She stabbed him four times, perhaps out of anger for all she'd been through. When it was done and his body was lifeless beside his mother, she collapsed to the ground, the knife falling to the ground. She stared at the gruesome scene that she'd created. She thought of the other horrific scene she'd seen not so long ago. The yellow dress ripped and splattered with red. The twisted angle of her neck. The bulging eyes.

It was too much. Suddenly, it was all too much. She crawled backward, away from the bodies, as if she could escape from the reality if she could put enough forested floor between them. She'd done something horrible, something worse than

Jade. He'd never forgive her now. Lilly would never understand, either. She'd lose everything.

It was Jade's fault. It was her fault. She'd done this. Wouldn't he see? Of course he wouldn't. He never did. He'd always defended her.

He loves her more.

The whispered phrase always in her head.

You're not as good of a mom.

The backup insult waiting to jump in at any moment, too.

She'd done it now. Jade would never bother them. Thad wouldn't be distracted by his first son. He'd have more time for Lilly. She just had to get away. Maybe they'd find Jade with Josh and assume she did it. She took the knife in her shaking hand, clutching it to her. And that was when she saw it. Near Jade, perhaps dropped in the battle, was the doll. She clutched at it like it was her true salvation, a winning ticket to a banquet she craved. She grabbed Evette, clutching her close. She rocked the doll for a long while, crying into her sweet body.

She was finally, shakily getting to her feet, though, when she heard more footsteps. Many this time. And when she turned to look toward the asylum, to see where to run, it was too late.

A sharp pinch bit into her arm. This time, the screams were all hers.

Chapter Thirty-Seven
Rose
Friday?

Tortured yells rattled through her aching head as she flicked her eyelids open. The blinding, migraine-inducing lights ricocheted off the white stone wall of the tiny cell she was in. Her body ached from the cement "cot" she was splayed on. She glanced down to see she was still in her jeans and sweatshirt. They already seemed like foreign ruins of a life gone by. Blood drenched her hands, congealed like gelatin on every rough centimeter of flesh. Rose turned her head slightly to the side and startled before relaxing. Sitting on the cot beside her was the doll, peacefully resting as if this was always meant to be her home. Evette. She gingerly claimed her, cradling the darling's head as her own started to spin. Her upper arm ached on her left side when she tried to create a crook for the precious angel, so she pulled the doll into her and hugged her against her chest with her right.

She felt woozy and energized as adrenaline pumped through her veins. She rocked the doll, embracing it to her tighter as tears fell. The thoughts came flooding in and devastating realizations flooded out.

She'd killed Jade. She'd killed Joshua. They were gone. Her life was over now. She'd done it to herself. What would become of her now? She perused the walls, the screams still echoing around her. She squeezed her eyes shut. This place, this house of horrors, would kill her. It was the most certain she'd ever been about anything She couldn't stay her. Certainly, Thad wouldn't let them keep her. . .

Oh, but he would. Once he found out what she'd done, he would let them lock her away, if he ever even found out where she was. Forget the trial. Forget the defense. She was a goner, a prisoner of this place she could already sense was twisted. She thought of the look in that woman's eyes, the relentless grip of the guards who held her down while they injected her. She looked around the windowless room and saw days and days stretched before. Her stomach churned. She wanted to die.

But that was nothing new. She'd wanted to die every day since that horrible incident, since her death. Since that bastard had mowed down her only daughter. Since she'd seen Lilly's yellow party dress drip with blood. Death would be her only savior now—but even that felt too far away to reach out and grasp. She clutched the doll closer, rocking back and forth as she sang Lilly's favorite lullaby. Her serenity and comfort were short lived, though. The cell door screeched open and slammed behind the woman.

"I see you're awake now," her sweet voice said. She wore her hair in braids, making her look innocent. Maybe she was, Rose thought. She hugged the doll closer.

Rose said nothing, staring at the woman. Another woman, a blonde, brought in a wheelchair.

"Where are we going?" Rose asked, her voice a muted whisper, a shell of the voice she used to possess. Terror started to climb through her veins and twist through her insides.

"We're going somewhere to help you," the nurse replied with a shrug.

"Who are you?"

"Anna. I'll be taking care of you now. Don't worry," she said, but the smile on her face read like a sinister grin. Tears fell. Rose wanted to go back. She wanted to go back to before Oakwood, before that psycho had killed her daughter and took off. Before the world was such a fucking mess. Before Thad stopped loving her. She wanted to go back to before, when the only thing she worried about was Jade, the psycho ex-wife, who seemed harmless now in the scheme of things. She wanted to go back to worrying about nursery colors and latte flavors and the taxes for her beauty salon.

She wanted to go back to when they'd moved in—what? Less than a week ago? She wanted to leave the doll in the garage. She wanted to shake Thad until he believed her that something was amiss. She wanted to get in her car, drive away, and never look back.

She would do anything to go back.

Rose glanced at the wheelchair and noticed splatters of blood on it. It seemed like a ridiculous thing to worry about considering the state of herself, but she was appalled by the sight of it. Good things did not happen to those in that wheelchair, she knew.

"I'm fine," she murmured, shaking her head and pulling back. Anna stepped forward.

"It's not a choice, Dear. We're going. Now get in." Her voice did not raise past a whisper, but the forceful energy behind her phrasing told Rose that it was, in fact, not a choice. The blonde nurse behind Anna studied her, holding her lips in a stoic, tight line.

Rose wanted to fight, to scream. But who would hear her? Who would care? She clutched Evette to her chest and stood, her legs wobbly. She tried not to think of the bloody wheelchair. Sobs ran down her face. She was a murderer. A mess. Maybe they could help her. Maybe this would be for the best.

The doll clung to her chest, her feeble arms hanging onto it for dear life. The nurse strapped her in the chair and wheeled her out of the room. How long had she been in the cell? She'd lost track of days, of time. She thought it had been a day, but maybe it had been longer. She wondered where Thad was now, if he had heard the news. She wondered what would become of him, a man who had lost everyone. His ex-wife, his son. His daughter. All dead. And her? She might as well be dead to him now, too.

The glaringly white lights stung her eyes as they wheeled her down the antiseptic hallway. Despite the fluorescence, it felt dim, dark, and dismal. They rolled her to the elevator, screams of agony punctuating the hallways. She couldn't stay here. She wouldn't. She clung to the doll, the nurses on either side as they waited for the elevator.

Down the hallway, another wheelchair screeched forward. The rider had long red hair that dangled in her face like a mask, black roots peeking through. She neared the elevator, and when the nurse pushing it stopped abruptly, the woman looked up. Her face was pale, her eyes shimmering as if from another world. Rose's stomach sank. It was as if she was looking in a mirror. She knew without asking. She knew.

Evette glanced at Rose, who stared back, hoping to wordlessly confide in her—what? But before she could even think to take stock of the situation, the woman's eyes landed on the doll in Rose's arms. She began violently flailing and screaming.

"Margot. Margot. Margot!" she yelled, her voice rabid with passion. She tried to stand up out of the wheelchair despite the strap, clutching for the doll that Rose pulled to herself tighter.

"That's my Margot! Sweet angel, Margot," she continued, raving like a madwoman she most definitely was. There was a scuffle of feet, a shuffling of wheelchairs and staff as the nurse retrieved the shot from her pocket and stabbed the other woman just in time. Tears fell from her eyes as she stared at Rose, whose chest rose and fell wildly with fear. After all had quieted and the drugs had kicked in, the elevator was summoned once more.

"Take the bitch back to her room. We'll take her down later," Anna barked at another nurse, who did as she was instructed and wheeled the seemingly lifeless woman to her room. Rose squinted, trying to ascertain whether or not she was still breathing.

The elevator bell rang out, a sickening, off-tune noise. They pushed Rose's wheelchair forward. Another nurse yelled to hold the elevator as a second wheelchair was pushed in, a blonde this time. Her blue eyes shimmered, but the bags under her eyes gave her skin an eerie, translucent quality. She was paper thin, see-through.

They stood in the elevator beside them, the two gate keepers beside their seated prey. No music rang out except for the muffled yells of the patients of the place. She wished it was all a dream. She prayed it was all a nightmare.

The doors opened. They had gone down, down, down. They pushed her wheelchair onto the new floor. It was cement, dusty, and dingy. There were a few bare bulbs here and there. Her heart sped up. Into a room both women were wheeled, and panic started to set in at the sight of medical equipment, stretchers, and a man in a lab coat.

Rose thought about screaming, about trying to fight her way out. She deserved to suffer, but the smell in the air told her this would be more than penance; it would be sheer torture she couldn't undo. Her eyes scanned the room as she tried to make a plan. But then the blonde beside her spoke. She'd been silent up until this point.

"You're here," she said, happiness flooding her voice. "Little yellow. I'm glad you're here. I am sorry, though. You know I'm sorry."

Rose turned to look to her companion's eyes. She followed the blonde's gaze to the corner of the room. And then, her heart palpitated with a similar feeling—joy. The medical equipment, the sheer terror, the atrocities awaiting her did not matter. Nothing mattered. Her heart swelled in a way it hadn't in months.

Her daughter. She stood there in her red braids and the yellow party dress. But it wasn't smattered with blood like last time. She stood there, shimmering and beautiful, her rosy cheeks full.

"Lilly," she whispered, tears filling her eyes. She tossed the doll off her lap as she reached out for her daughter, her sweet, sweet angel.

Her red braids. Her yellow dress.

Her daughter stepped forward.

"It's okay, Mommy," the sweet girl whispered. Lilly stroked her hair now, and Rose closed her eyes. If a mother's love could've saved her. If only a mother's love could've been enough.

"I'm sorry," the blonde woman beside her said, and Rose wanted to ask why. She wanted to know how. She wanted to ask the doctor who was stepping forward what would happen to her. But as her daughter stood at her side, she knew it didn't matter.

If a mother's love could only have saved her child. She loved her hard enough, didn't she? It didn't matter anymore. The doctor wheeled her forward, toward the stretcher. Her vision started to blur.

All she could see was yellow, but her heart radiated for the first time in months.

She was home now.

Chapter Thirty-Eight
Evette

I awaken in my cell with a splitting migraine and a fleeting memory of being the hallway. They were taking me somewhere. I had heard bad things about the basement place and what happened when you went there. Nothing could be worse, though, than the suffering I've endured these past months—years? I don't know anymore.

And then, it hits me. Everything starts spinning as my mind settles on the truth. It wasn't a dream. It happened.

Margot. The woman was holding Margot. My sweet, angel girl. I thought I'd never see her again. But she was in the hallway. She is in the building now. There's still a chance for me to get her back.

I was foolish, it's true. I'd let my emotions get the best of me. But where did I go wrong? Was it coming to Oakwood after John's death? Certainly, that wasn't the wisest course of action looking back now. I should have kept moving. Settling is always a risk in these situations. But I wanted to build a life for Margot, one of stability and peace. And that house I'd rented along the woods was a perfect sanctuary. Oh, how she loved going for strolls at the forest's edge in the mornings. How we found peace there.

Was it that I wanted too much? Maybe. Perhaps that's always been my tragic flaw. I've always needed more than I deserved. I've always grasped for the stars when I should've been happy with the ground.

I wanted to give Margot a sister. Was that so bad? It's all I ever wanted—to be a mother. And after I settled into that house at 312 Cedar Lane, I knew it was the perfect time. And so I'd watched. I'd waited. I'd done my research.

Fucking Janice. Always so smug in that coffee shop, always rubbing her belly in front of me like a magic eight ball. Always walking by in her too-high heels—who wears stilettos in the eighth month of pregnancy? Don't you care about your child at all?—and always grinning at me with Margot, as if she was so much better. But she'd got hers. I'm smart, much smarter than they all thought. And so, I'd figured out how to get into the hospital. This stupid town isn't careful with protocol, after all. I'd found the entrance. I'd stolen the ID badge. And then I waited for her due date. I waited for the perfect moment to strike—and I'd made my getaway.

It would have worked, too—except for that freaking new girl at the hospital. Of course, she got lost when I was heading down the stairs. Of course, she was right where I was making my exit.

I didn't mean for it to happen. I didn't. I don't want to talk about that part, about the sweet angel. It was her fault. If she hadn't been in the way. If she'd have left me go by, we'd be living in another town.

It's not my fault. It isn't.

After it happened, I didn't have time to think. I knew what it would look like. I had to get away so that I could be with Margot. I shoved the nurse down the steps, but it wasn't a hard enough fall to kill her or even knock her out. Perhaps that was my biggest mistake. She sounded the alarm. I was finished. My dreams were gone, and that poor, sweet baby was stuck being raised by that slut Janice.

I'd thought I'd go to jail—which wouldn't do. The police had to be looking for me after John's situation. However, I should've known that Oakwood does things so differently. Always so different.

And here I am, in this wretched place where no one will find me and everyone loathes me. I'm the crazy baby stealer. I'm the murderer, as they've figured out. I'm nothing but a tortured mind they can torture some more. There is so much evil in this world. I'd known it all along, tried to protect Margot from it. But sometimes a mother's love isn't enough.

It's hard, but at least I know she's here. And hopefully that woman will keep her safe. It's been my biggest regret that after getting caught, I didn't get to go back and get her. I would have done anything to go back and get her. And oh, how I've tried.

I've had time to think. It was a rotten plan. I would have never been able to stay with that baby. The town is too small. I was foolish. I was an idiot. John always thought so. Maybe he was right.

I've gotten used to this place, though, in some ways. I miss Margot, of course. But maybe this is where I belong. After all, I've found my children in a way. This place is filled with them. So many kids. Hurt, abandoned, lonely. Wandering the halls, a wispy specter of who they should be. Who mistreated them?

Who left them here? They do not speak of it, but they come to me at night. They don't say anything but they're there. And I love them as if they were my own.

There are worse mothers than me, after all.

Chapter Thirty-Nine
Thad

He should've known it was too much, should have fought harder to make sure she was getting help. He should have had her committed like everyone back in town had told him. And now, both of his children were dead.

Lilly's death from a hit and run driver was devastating for him, too. He'd fallen into a pit of despair—but the difference was, he'd had to pick himself out of it. He'd had no choice. The family depended on him, and he always rose to the challenge. Even if it meant shoving aside his own sorrow over his murdered child.

But Rose had never recovered. Motherhood was her defining attribute, her identity. When that car slaughtered their little girl, it eviscerated everything that had kept her whole. He'd thought the move would help, getting away from the space where it happened. Getting away from Jade, who was always lurking in the corners of Rose's hurting mind. He thought he'd done the right thing. And now both of his kids were dead.

The woman he'd loved, tried to love whole again, had murdered them all.

Jade was gone, a woman he once shared a life with. Lilly was gone. Josh was gone. All gone.

And now she was worse than dead to him to.

He could've forgiven her for Jade. The police had told him about a van set up in the woods, about how she'd been there for a while. He shuddered to think that Rose had clearly beat Jade at her own game. But he would never forgive her for Josh. He would never, ever forgive her. In fact, he never wanted to see her again.

The police in Oakwood had been more than helpful. They'd taken care of the bodies, helped him organize a small funeral for just their immediate families. They'd assured him after investigating that they would take care of Rose, that he wouldn't have to deal with her. They promised she'd finally get the help she needed. He wanted to be thankful for that, be appreciative they weren't sending her straight to the dungeon of the max penitentiary in the state but to an asylum, a place where her mental state could be evaluated. He didn't have the fortitude to deal with a trial. He didn't want to see her.

After it all settled, though, he didn't feel relief or anger or anything, really. He felt numb. Dead. Cold.

His mother was staying with him. Suicide watch, apparently. She'd thought him to be well enough to go to the grocery store for a little while and gather casserole supplies. Perhaps that was her mistake. Life wasn't full of choices, like some supposed. It was a series of mistakes, of missteps, that led to your demise. The house sat cold, empty, silent. He inhaled the stagnant air. He breathed out what was left of his will to survive.

They were all gone. Rose would spend her days in Redwood. Moving there had been a mistake. It was all a mistake, his entire life. He'd tried so hard to be a man his father would've been proud of. Instead, he was a fucking disaster.

He climbed up on the chair and tugged on the rope to make sure it was tight, ready. He looked out the sliding glass doors into the wilderness, thought about his life, and put the rope around his neck.

His last thought wasn't of her, like he always thought it would be.

His last image wasn't of his son, who he missed so much, or his daughter in her bright, yellow dress.

For some reason, which he didn't have time to ponder, his last thought was of the doll, it's eerie expression and lifelike features. He kicked off the chair and felt pain indescribable as he breathed his last breath of sheer and utter torture.

Epilogue

It was the doll, they would say, if the world knew of Evette Harding and Rose Taylor. Something was wickedly wrong with that angelic body. Perhaps they would write lore about where it came from or how it was cursed by some immortal entity. Some would create stories with Ouija boards and bad spirits. Some would compare it to that infamous doll and lock it away in a museum for all to see and no one to touch. Clearly, something about that doll is what sparked the evil.

Others would blame a world where women were less, where mothering was put above else. They would blame the husbands who both were narcissistic in their own ways. Who convinced their spouses that love would save them and domestic bliss was their ultimate fulfillment. Some would say John got what he deserved, and that Thad deserved even worse.

Some would say that the two women were sick, the victims of mental illnesses misunderstood.

Some would say they were twisted, rotten at the core. Some would say darkness lurks in all.

Others would blame circumstance and upbringings. They would see similarities in their stories and darkness in their deeds.

Still others would say that some women cling so fiercely to motherhood that without it, they go quite mad.

No one can really know for sure, though. They can only speculate, as we always do in these horrible tales. For the world would not know of the women. The world would not piece them together. Their cases would grow cold in those stone cells filled with solitude and nightmares from the past. Redwood would make sure of that. For with the other criminally insane, rejected, people from the frays of society, the two would suffer at the hands of the haunted halls, day and night. They would be locked away, forgotten, just like Oakwood likes it. They would fade away from existence, becoming shells of people—until the keeper decided otherwise. Until their true value in the asylum, their true roles, became clear. And by then, it would be too late. Just like it was for the others, it would be far too late.

The only memory of them? The doll left behind in a cold cell, fighting waves of loneliness as well. Her only company would be the ghosts of those who had suffered in the wicked ways of the stone walls. She would bear witness to the lingering ghost of those who had died but never left. Redwood doesn't permit that, after all.

Until then, Evette and Rose wait—for redemption, for insanity, for something that won't come. Many would argue that Jade was the one who got off easy.

For maybe it's the futile waiting that does it, after all.

Or maybe it's something else entirely.

Whatever it is, we do know this: We're all one delivery, one choice, one fatal swipe of a knife away from a completely twisted future.

Choose wisely, dear friend.

Always choose wisely.

Acknowledgements

First, I want to thank all of my readers who have picked up my books, read my stories, and given a small-town girl's dreams a chance. I couldn't do this without all of you and your support. Sometimes, this author journey is lonely and hard, but you all inspire me to keep going.

Thank you to my amazing agent, Erica, at Metamorphosis Literary Agency for believing in my work and helping me dream bigger dreams.

I also want to thank my husband, who always encourages me to tell the stories on my heart and "Write for the wolves." I love you so much for being there for me, for encouraging me, and for listening to all of my crazy ideas. You're my best friend forever.

Thank you to my parents for instilling a love of learning, reading, and writing in me at a young age. You taught me the power of words and dreams.

Thank you to all of my friends, family, teachers, and co-workers who have supported me on this journey. I am so blessed to have so many people in my corner.

And thank you to Edmund, my newest writing companion who is much more distracting than Henry but supportive all the same. You make me laugh even when I feel like crying, and I love you for that.

About the Author

L.A. Detwiler is a USA Today Bestselling author of thriller and horror novels. Her debut thriller, The Widow Next Door, was published with HarperCollins Uk/Avon Books. The Diary of a Serial Killer's Daughter won the bronze medal for psychological thriller from Readers' Favorite.

L.A. is a high school English teacher in her hometown in Pennsylvania. She is married to her junior high sweetheart. They have six rescued cats and a mastiff named Henry, who appears in all of her works. She loves shopping, chocolate, Starbucks, and *Outlander*. She dreams of meeting Sam Heughan, so if anyone has any strings they can pull...just kidding. Not kidding...

Email: authorladetwiler@gmail.com

Blog: www.ladetwiler.com[1]

Facebook: www.facebook.com/ladetwiler[2]

Sign-up for L.A. Detwiler's VIP reader's club for FREE and get a FREE copy of her short story, "I'd Kill for You" as a thank-you: https://dl.bookfunnel.com/bx3spg4ri7

---

1.   http://www.ladetwiler.com

2.   http://www.facebook.com/ladetwiler

The dead do talk...if you're brave enough to listen.

Read on for a sample from my paranormal horror, The Redwood Asylum.[1]

---

1. https://www.amazon.com/gp/product/
B08BDDSW92

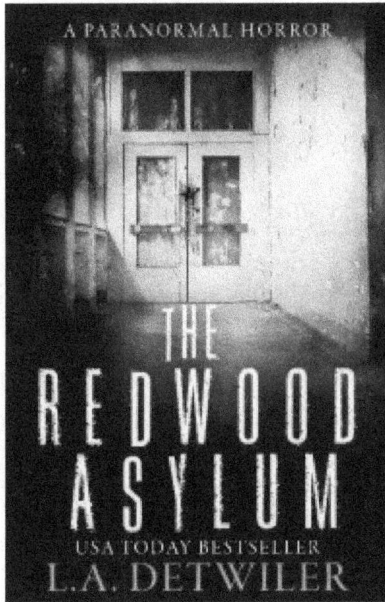

Prologue

On a winding road, concealed in a dark forest of overpowering trees and forgotten memories, sits a seemingly ancient building. The town it belongs to, Oakwood, likes to forget its existence, but the prisoners harbored behind the decaying stone walls know very much what the place is. Not many places like it have subsisted in its form, but since 1834, the Redwood Asylum has stood proud and tall, welcoming its patients in and feasting on whatever remains of their mental states.

It began with good intentions in 1834, if misguided by the cruel realities of medicine at the time. Francis Weathergate's sister, Claudette, was struggling with what medical doctors deemed nervous conditions due to her melancholic behaviors, tantrums, and risk-taking penchants. In modern times, medical doctors would deem her a teenager, but the era was different. We cannot always fault people for being who they are in the time they are born into.

The son of a wealthy mine owner, Francis did what he knew to do—he threw money at the problem, building the most state-of-the-art, five-story facility dedicated to asylum medicine of the time. And for a while, Redwood, from the exterior, was a picturesque building one could smile at, a sort of vacation home quality permeating every facet of its existence. The wealthy felt good about locking up the members of their families labeled inferior. The outside was glossy, picture-worthy, and stunning.

But as with all facilities of this nature, the interior was a horror that couldn't be so readily masked. Some said if you got too close, you could hear the screams of not only the living. The deceased inhabitants supposedly strolled aimlessly through the thick forest at night, stuck in Redwood's claws even after death. Some said their minds were too far gone to even know when to die. Others still thought maybe something was amiss at Redwood but of course didn't worry enough to investigate. After all, they were ten miles away in the town center, drinking coffee and chasing dollars and feeling the warm sunshine on their pale faces. Thus, the town went quiet, leaving the asylum to its dark devices in the midst of its forest island so far on the outskirts of town, it was practically its very own.

Today, Redwood Asylum would be a tourist attraction, a place for the photographer to visit, to smile in front of, to garnish attention. But Oakwood already has plenty of money, so it prefers to keep Redwood somewhat of a secret, a forgotten relic of the past that is still functioning. In fact, if you were to visit Oakwood, you would not hear a whisper about the building with a maniacal interior. And even if you stumbled upon the building, you may not even realize that the prisoners still remain—both living and dead.

Certainly, the sign out front has been transformed from The Redwood Asylum to The Redwood Psychiatric Center, a play on words that sounds more pleasing to the ear of the mentally stable. But make no mistake—the residents, as they're now called formally, know exactly what the sign out front should say. And the residents of the past know exactly what the current residents should expect.

The nurses and staff at Redwood aren't evil monsters. No, most are simply desperate for work or desperate to disappear from the world in a sense. Some are eager to remind themselves that they are of the mentally sound side, and there's nothing like working with the most intense mentally disturbed cases to do just that.

Still, this living artifact carries with it an evil past and an equally as frightening future. For once inside, the criminally insane, the darkly disturbed, and the eternally confused residents learn one thing very quickly: they are now at the mercy of others.

If you know anything about human nature, you know that mercy rarely overstays its welcome.

Did you love *Evette: A Domestic Thriller*? Then you should read *The Flayed One*[2] by L.A. Detwiler!

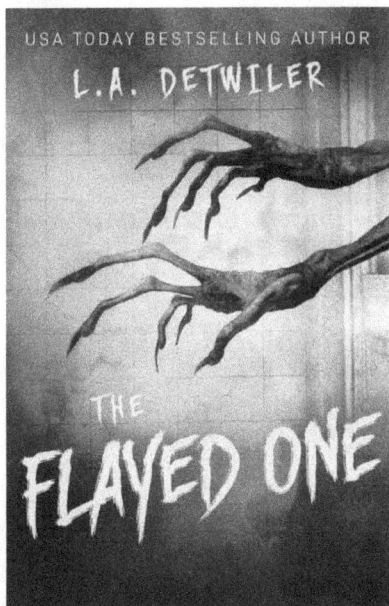

It comes at night, when the world is a dusty, quiet ball of forgotten memories. The thing of shrieks, of shrill, wanton fears makes its presence known. At seventeen, Mia Rose Ellis is haunted by a tragic summer and painful secrets. Seeking refuge in the forest behind her house, however, she finds two things that change everything: a rotten corpse and an archaic journal filled with horrifying tales. As Mia begins to read the eerie stories of a terrifying, malicious creature, she begins to realize the forest surrounding her house is more dangerous than she could've imagined.***Its origins are the whispered legends of the curious, carved on victims' hearts.*** The town of Oakwood, home to the infamous Redwood Asylum, has always harbored its own sinister enigmas. The journal, however, launches Mia into a world where legends become reality and the frights of the forest follow her home. Will Mia be able to find the help she needs to survive The Flayed One's malicious hunting game, or will she be its next victim? ***For when the Flayed One comes for you, make no mistake.*** ***You will not be saved.*** *From USA Today Bestseller L.A. Detwiler comes a hot new creature horror series sure to give you nightmares.*

Read more at www.ladetwiler.com.

Also by L.A. Detwiler

Maternal Instincts
Evette: A Domestic Thriller

The Flayed One
The Journal of H.D. Wards
The Flayed One

Standalone
The Diary of a Serial Killer's Daughter
A Tortured Soul
The Christmas Bell: A Horror Novel
The Redwood Asylum
The Christmas Bell: Rachel's Story
The Arsonist's Handbook
Mr. Alexander Garrick's Traveling Circus
The Butcher's Night
The Witch of War Creek
The Delivery

Teaching High School Creative Writing

Watch for more at www.ladetwiler.com.

CPSIA information can be obtained
at www.ICGtesting.com
Printed in the USA
BVHW042100270522
638324BV00004B/41

9 798201 847777